Gidjie

and the
Wolves

Gidjie
and the
Wolves

THE
INTERMEDIARIES
VOLUME ONE
by Tashia Hart

Dedication

This book is dedicated to all children; the young and the young at heart. Let us speak words and commit to actions that uplift and free one another always.

Contents

Prologue

When humans first began to walk the Earth, they were looked upon in curiosity by the preceding bipeds of the era. Unlike the older bipeds, who were capable of assuming both animal and human-like forms, the new humans had no tails, feathers, fangs, or fur to speak of.

The older, dual-natured beings became known as the Intermediaries, and they took upon themselves the duty of watching over humans and animals alike.

Over time, a communication gap grew between the humans and the other beings. This led to confusion and, unfortunately, hostile behavior.

Brief warfare occurred between the Intermediaries and the humans, and the Intermediaries—many who were more powerful in physical form than the humans—soon became regretful of the damage they had inflicted.

As a result, they decided to hide their dual nature, and only present themselves in human-like form when interacting with the human beings.

Over the years, the customs and cultures of the Intermediaries developed to bridge the communication gap between animals and humans, and they continue to work hard in their position of service to both accordingly.

The goal of the average Intermediary in present day, is to help cultivate a space in time where all of the beings can understand one another clearly.

This story is about a human girl, adopted into a family of Intermediaries. Immersed in this hidden world, she seeks to understand where she fits in, and what her role will be.

Three Stories Down, Not Up

The baking floor is on the third story down—not up, beneath the gentle piney-sway of a boreal forest nestled near the shore of Gichigami.*

Above ground, late spring is abloom with an abundance of white forest flowers. Below however, we arrive into our story, beneath moss and humus, stone and root, into the season of the young councils.

Just like everything that is born, grows and lives in harmony with Maamaa Aki, the Earth, the Intermediaries have a rhythm to their coming of age. Setting off to form one's council of peers is the first step towards self-determination.

During this time of year, the head of every young Intermediary in the Northern Hemisphere is in a tizzy— for any moment might be the one to start them off on their adventure.

Their nervousness and anticipation are understandable, as a council is a bond and station that lasts a lifetime.

As it happens, the head of one—just one—young human is also preoccupied with such matters.

*Gichigami means 'a large lake' and more specifically, refers to Lake Superior.

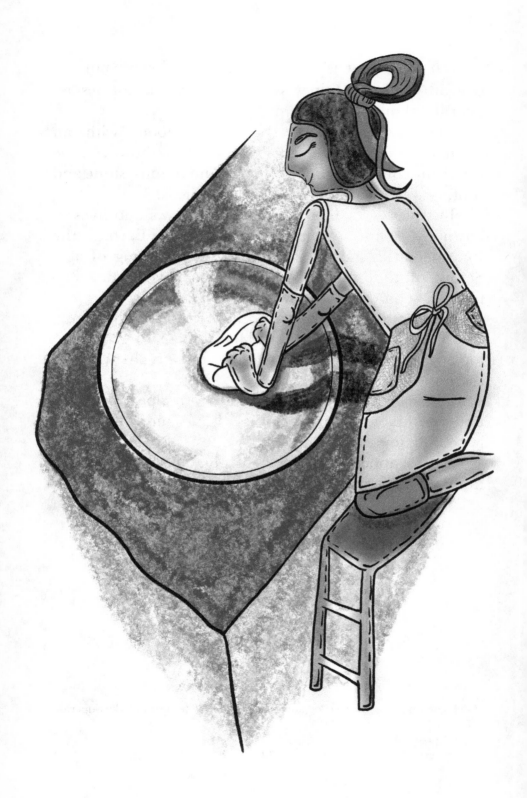

We find Gidjie in her favorite knee-length, bright red dress with a nettle-twine apron tied at her waist. A flat, square stone, black on one side and white on the other, hangs about her neck. And the humming. She is humming a very old hum, the kind that makes slime molds ooze and sway this way and that; the kind that can make water ripple—if ever just so slightly. Her black, waist-long hair is pinned on the top of her head, and she is covered nearly head to toe in light-blue mineral dust.

This oughta do the trick. This time, it'll work for sure, she thinks to herself as she kneads gingerly.

She holds up the little piece of dough, looking proudly at it for a moment, before slipping it into the glass jar that sits in her shoulder bag beside her.

She wipes her hands on a towel and gives them a good loud CLAP! before digging into one of the pockets of her apron. She pulls them out, and they are bright green.

She climbs onto the bench next to her and reaches out, picking up the dough-ball that was crawling towards the edge of the counter. She pulls it towards her and into the clean basin.

She pauses her humming to look straight down at the dough she is now kneading.

"Oh, I don't know Bluebelle. *If* I was permitted, and *if* it was anything like what aunt Flaurinzia does, I could wind up just about anywhere," she says, trying hard to imagine the future, "*if* I wasn't a human, of course."

A few bubbles pop up from the surface of the dough-ball named Bluebelle.

"That's true, some people find themselves closer to home, like aunt Molandoras. But she never seems happy. I suspect that's the reason she's aged faster than Flaurinzia, but who knows."

Gidjie resumes kneading Bluebelle in the carved-into-the-stone-counter basin.

"You're right, Molandoras is characteristically pessimistic about nearly everything, not just her work," she sighs, "I really am perfectly happy right here with you and Nookomis."

It is in the next moment, that she finds herself making a declaration to stop the curiosity of these 'what-ifs,' "I will live here for the rest of my life, with you and Nookomis, working in the shop like I always have. And I do have Carver," her brow furrows the moment the words come out.

Carver is like Gidjie's adoptive family—he's an Intermediary. She can't bear to think about being without his company if—when—he is called off to form his council.

More bubbles from Bluebelle and Gidjie can't help but smile, "Yes, I know I'm your favorite human," a pause and then, "Of course you're my favorite dough-ball."

Bluebelle is in fact the only living dough-ball Gidjie knows, but after years of her questioning, she can't help but wonder if there might be others out there.

She also can't help but wonder—with the right recipe, is it possible to *create* one, so that Bluebelle might have a companion?

In an attempt to answer that question, Gidjie has been spending long nights working on such a recipe and wondering about the properties the dough might have when baked into bread.

She looks to the glass jar in her shoulder bag that holds the little piece of dough, and smiles.

The most prominent feature on the baking floor is a cluster of 7 ovens, each large enough to hold a dozen loaves of bread at a time.

Atop every carved stone dome lives a gem the size of a large dinner plate, that shines brightly when the bread inside reaches peak deliciousness—and potential, for that matter.

Let it be known that not all fires are the same. Those that dwell in these particular ovens are of individual natures.

If you had the good fortune to look down from above upon fires and gems aglow, you might believe you were peering into an illuminated corner of space, for the glimmering cluster resembles a gathering of stars.

Truth be told, one might also say the ovens appear arranged haphazardly. Story has it, Gidjie's adoptive grandfather, being an unusually large and excitable rabbit, had ran around digging fire pits for the first time in his life, when his newly wedded wife had pondered, "Where shall I do my baking?" The stone ovens were a later addition, built where the original pits had been.

"Gidjie, I'm ready for Bluebelle," the voice of her grandmother arrives from the little stone grate on the far side of the room.

"Coming, Nookomis," she answers, looking down at the bounding-back-in-to-shape dough-ball who's starting to ripple and casually wander off again.

"Okay Bluebelle, it's time," she addresses her. She reaches out her hands. Bluebelle turns to meet Gidjie's gentle embrace.

Gidjie hops down from the stool and carries Bluebelle across the wide, circular baking floor, passing through several of the wind rush areas. These are places where drafts are constantly upwelling from deep within the Earth, and up, up, into the levels above and outwards to the forest floor. If you were above ground and happened to witness the expulsion, you'd probably assume that the ground was settling, or a fish was gurgling, or that it was simply an average discharge of the wind. However, the peculiar smells that can accompany these discharges, might leave you second-guessing.

On her way to the door, Gidjie stops to plunge an arm elbow-deep into a hanging weaverbird basket. Her aunt Flaurinzia had brought back several of these baskets from the island where she lives and works most of the year.

Weaverbirds, having exceptionally nimble feet, weave the baskets out of volcanic-gas-cured squid tentacles. They hunt the squids and then hang them to dry, deep in the volcano they inhabit. The baskets are special, for they hold a perpetual heat.

What does an underground-dwelling, grandmother-granddaughter baking-team-extraordinaire, store in such a basket, you might ask?

18

She pulls out a green, glowing cube.

"And throw more peat in the oven on your way over please," Nookomis adds.

Gidjie smiles and walks over to the green-gem-adorned oven. She tosses the little cube to the flames.

As they slowly make their way down the hall towards the rising room, Gidjie stops to admire the way the ancient, carved-in-stone-stories that line the hallway, are illuminated by the flickering light of the baking room. Shadows cast by the ridges in the carvings, dance and play, and pay visit to each other from the corner of her eye.

Nookomis' voice sounds in the near distance, "I saw what looked like a dead opossum on the fourth floor."

Gidjie grins wide, "We haven't had one of those in a while," she says.

Opossums
Make the Best

Best Friends

"Carver, is that you?" Gidjie lifts her head an inch to give the slightest glance in the direction of the commotion. She knows it's him. It's always him.

A pink nose pops up above the counter across from her. Then a long furry snout, with teeth poking out each side. Finally, an entire furry head is sitting there.

"Hey Gidjie, did you finish it yet?" Carver asks, notably hungry.

"Oh good. It's my opossum friend, Carver," she says, avoiding his question on purpose.

"Very funny. So, did you?"

"And he's *alive*," she adds, giving him a stare.

"Your grandmother startled me this morning," he says before turning to look over his shoulder, "Sorry about that, Nookomis."

Nookomis doesn't seem to hear him, as she is minding to Bluebelle in a large, dry basin built into the floor of the rising room nearby. It is of sufficient size and depth so as to completely conceal the goings-on within.

Vents along the bottom of the basin, provide warm airflow, allowing for the quick rise of Bluebelle's many forms of dough.

Nearly-neon-green, floury dust is flying up in poofs from out of sight every little while, accentuating the air.

They can hear Nookomis talking to Bluebelle, getting her ready for her rise. A quiet lullaby begins. It is a song of love and thanks.

Bluebelle has given many loaves of bread over the course of her lifetime, and for every loaf of bread, she works hard to rebuild her dough stock.

Why, at this very moment, while Bluebelle is here in the rising room, she is *also* in the incubator room, enjoying recuperation time with special minerals and spices to keep her healthy and growing until her next divide.

It is an old arrangement, this giving and receiving of companionship, love, and bread between her and them. One that Gidjie isn't aware the origin of, given she's never had the notion to ask about such things.

Just out of sight, Nookomis is sporting a slick suit with a hood and rainbow-colored goggles. Covered in oil, and slippery but for her boots—she is kneading Bluebelle as she rises.

Gidjie loves that job. It's fun to bounce and do belly flops on Bluebelle as she grows. It always feels a little like a farewell party however, for once Bluebelle reaches her peak rise, she takes on a more regular dough-like form.

The task of rising Bluebelle isn't suited for Nookomis' animal form of blue jay—at least not yet. The part that *is* suited for a bird, is one of Gidjie's favorite things to watch her grandmother do. But it's not time for that yet.

Her attention is brought back to Carver, "I'm sure you probably startled her too, seeing how she found you dead on the fourth floor," she says, stalling the answering of the original question he had asked.

She wasn't actually upset for any other reason than the fact Carver has always had more access to the fourth floor where the Ancient Traders Market is.

The fourth floor is also home to the middle door, as well as the trade tunnels that lie on the other side of the door and extend into the beyond Gidjie has never stepped foot in.

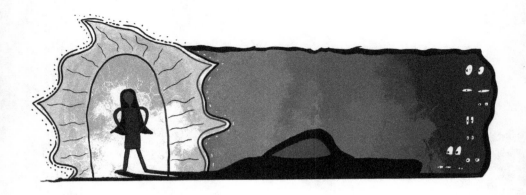

She knows she shouldn't get mad at him for it. It's not his fault she's human and has thus far been forbidden to use the middle door. She would get less upset however, if he weren't always brushing her off about what's in the tunnels when she inquires. He doesn't seem to think it's a big deal she's never been beyond the middle door, and his answers are usually along the lines of, "It's just tunnels and spiders and stuff."

"Again, sorry," he says, his little furry hand reaching up onto the counter to grab at things before turning his palm upwards in question, "but what about that dough?"

"Which one would that be again?" she raises an eyebrow and looks up to the ceiling, feigning a memory lapse, but unable to stop a smile from creeping across her face.

The dough in question isn't ready yet, but she's not about to tell him that. Not with all of her previous boasting about being so close. And not that she's ever been one to boast—she just really wanted to get it right— but hasn't. Yet.

"You know, the one you've been working on all winter, and all spring and is finally, *finally* ready to go into the oven. That's what you said yesterday. And the day before, and the day before, and it would be really great if I could get a taste sooner than later…"

"What were you doing down there, anyway?" Gidjie interrupts him mid-pestering, getting the feeling there's something he's not telling her.

Being that she's only ever allowed on the fourth floor when there's a delivery too big for Nookomis to handle alone, she's genuinely curious. When she is allowed down there on such occasions to wait by the middle door, she tries her best to get a good look at whoever the delivery person is, and anything notable about them.

"Uhmm…tail fishing?" he says with a toothy, nervous smile, holding up the tip of his tail.

Gidjie leans forward to inspect it for bite marks, which would be a sure sign he'd been using his tail as bait.

"But then I got tired," he drops his tail before she can get a good look, "and your house was closer than mine, so I thought I would…"

His weird behavior makes her give him a good sideways squint, but she moves on, "Thought you would scare an old woman?"

A skittish chuckle pops out of his lips, that tighten quickly to contain it.

She reaches across the counter to wipe a little flour on the tip on his nose. He sneezes mightily. Flour flies up and settles onto both of their faces.

They laugh until their sides hurt, pointing at each other, and decide not to pressure the other to talk about the things they obviously don't want to talk about.

A Few Things
About Intermediaries

To most humans, opossum Carver looks like just that, an opossum. Nothing more, nothing less. To Gidjie, however, he looks like an opossum—standing a little above her knee—but with *movement* inside of him. Or, at least that's how she's explained it to him. In human form, he's barely a smidgen taller than her.

She's not sure why or how she sees Intermediaries in this way. Maybe it's because she's grown up around them. In any case, it's fun to watch them doing things in animal form. Like now.

Gidjie can't help but laugh in delight at the appearance of her grandmother, who's reached the part of the rising process suited for a bird.

She soars
up out of the basin,
a few feet higher
than the rim,

before
turning
back
into
human
form,

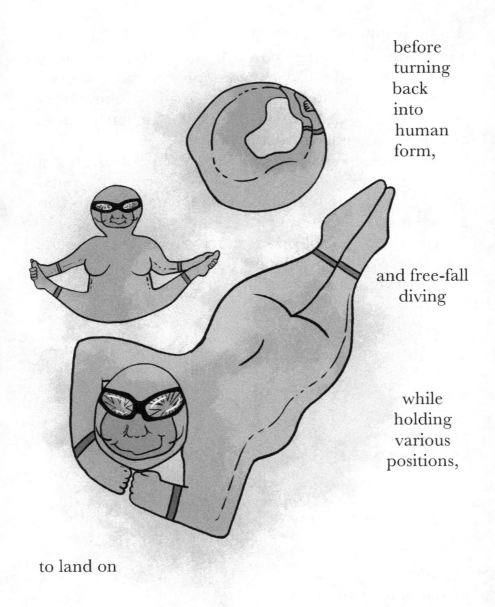

and free-fall
diving

while
holding
various
positions,

to land on

and better
knead

Bluebelle.

"Hey, that's a new shirt," Gidjie tells Carver, noticing how nicely made it is. His mother has made a few clothing items for Gidjie over the years, including her favorite red dress, which fits more like a long shirt these days.

Carver's family members are mostly raccoons. They live in a giant, hollow-yet-still-alive tree near Gidjie's house, with a nice burrow extending underground, safely tucked among the roots. They also have access to the trade tunnels by means of the deepest arm of their burrow.

A few years ago, she had tried following him into his home—at his request—to play. To make a long story short, 3 raccoons and a passer-by badger had to dislodge her from the tree by pulling her out by the ankles. She remembers the day clearly because of the incident, but also because afterwards, an assembly of sapsuckers—who no one had noticed were watching the ordeal—had flown off in a black and white and red all over ruckus after she was freed. Anyhow, she's been nervous of tight places ever since.

When Carver and his mother arrive together at Gidjie's home for a visit, they greet the household in formal custom, by announcing themselves with a tune on the melody stones beside the middle door, and then wait to be attended.

Many of the doors in the Between World* have such musical devices; whether percussion, wind or some other particular family favorite. Intermediary families along the trade tunnels, maintain melodies unique to their family, that are used to verify a person's identity and whereabouts.

* The upper underground that is connected by trade tunnels. As opposed the Below World, which is much, much deeper.

To his mother's chagrin, Carver is less formal on his daily solo visits. He likes to sneak in through gaps in earth and stone in the trade tunnels that only he knows about, emerging on the fourth floor before making his way to find Gidjie. Other times, he'll scramble in from the forest floor of the Above World* by means of abandoned animal dens and tunnels. In any case, he's made a game out of finding new ways in over the years.

"Carver—that you?" Nookomis says from atop a giggling and ever expanding Bluebelle, who has risen high enough so Nookomis can see them over the rim of the basin.

"Hi Nookomis, sorry about earlier," he blushes, being embarrassed anytime he gets discovered mid-sneak.

"What?" Nookomis says, rolling back and forth, digging her elbows into the now ginormous dough-ball.

"It's always him, Nookomis. He says he's sorry," Gidjie raises the volume of her voice a bit.

"Tell him his mother's looking for him."

"She always is," Gidjie looks at Carver, who shrugs.

His mom's recently taken to making a habit of constantly worrying about him. Apparently, unusual visitors have been stopping by at all hours of the night to try and pay him a visit. She thinks they're trying to… well, Gidjie's not exactly sure what his mother thinks, but she's got *her* suspicions. *She* assumes it has to do with Carver getting called off to form a council, and his mother's worried something bad might come of it.

*The level of the Earth that humans inhabit.

Like what happened to their parents. Carver's father went missing around the same time Gidjie's mom and dad disappeared.

When questioned about their parents, all Nookomis says is, "Good people," and that she misses them. She says even less about her estranged husband, Gidjie's adoptive grandfather, whom Gidjie doesn't remember ever meeting.

Gidjie and Carver have sat together many a time, trying to recollect things about their parents. It was so long ago, that neither recalls what they looked like. Gidjie sometimes dreams of her parents' voices, but that's about it.

Change

"Take Carver on the lift with you when you go okay, so his mother doesn't get upset about him not using proper doors like she did last week," Nookomis tells Gidjie.

"You know he can hear you, Nookomis?" Gidjie inquires, as Carver is standing nearby, but her grandmother isn't addressing him directly.

"I'm sorry, Carver," she says, "I've been having a hard time hearing your quiet opossum voice lately and I'm afraid it's getting worse. I might need a good ear cleaning." She grabs and rolls up a piece of birch bark lying next to the basin and sticks it to her ear like an ear candle, while making an exaggerated face expressing strained listening.

They laugh.

"Are you having a hard time hearing anything else?" Gidjie continues her query.

"It's normal for things to change, older ya get," Nookomis replies, giving her a curious side eye.

A long moment passes, and Gidjie begins to wonder if her grandmother is talking about herself, or if she's now talking about Gidjie, "In fact, it's normal for things to change your entire life. Be weird if they didn't, I reckon. As for my ears, I got something coming that'll fix'em right up."

Carver gives Nookomis a look of amusement and Gidjie trails off in thought, her gaze settling on Bluebelle, who was changing right before her eyes.

"How old is Bluebelle?" she wonders aloud.

"Well, let's see," Nookomis is standing next to the basin, holding a bucketful of glowing, green powder. She flings it up, vivid green cascading all about the top of the ever-rising Bluebelle.

She climbs onto her and begins rubbing the powder vigorously, as if the motion of it is helping her remember.

"She's been in the family 100 years, plus or minus mhphfhhmphfh," her answer tapers off inaudibly, as she drops deep into thought.

"Plus or minus…*what?*" Gidjie asks. Nookomis has always had a hard time answering questions relating to the tracking of time in a linear fashion.

"It was around the human year 1870 when your grandfather brought her home to me, hoping I'd be able to nurse her back to health. She came to me in the form of a dough that was being fried, during a hard time for the Anishinaabeg. I suspect before that, she lived multiple lifetimes as various dough-balls. As you know, they take on different forms depending on how they're fed, as is the case with this here batch of dough," she says, tenderly patting the top of Bluebelle, "It takes a lot to change a dough-ball's nature entirely though, as our Bluebelle's always alive in the variations we help shape her into."

Gidjie notes that it is currently the human year of 2020 and is about to ask where the other 50 years in Bluebelle's timeline went since 1870, when Carver steers the conversation.

"Wow," he says, "Bluebelle's older than my mom."

"How old is your mom, anyway?" Gidjie asks him, her last question lost as her curiosity about his mother takes over. Carver and Gidjie are both 11, and she takes comfort in hearing about his mom. It makes her feel a little closer to her own mother, in a way. It's not often he talks about her. He doesn't like to rub it in Gidjie's face that he has a mom.

"I think she's…80, but that's a guess. She's said she's 36 with every full change of seasons, and has for as long as I can remember."

"Your mother's well over 100," Nookomis chimes in, now standing next to them at the counter, "She's nearly half my age."

35

Gidjie and Carver gasp in unison; both at the reveal of Carver's mom's age, and also because they've never heard Nookomis suggest at her own age in terms of numbers before. She'd usually say she was as old as a tree, or as young as a spry jellyfish, or something along those lines.

"So, you're at least 200? Is that a normal age for an Intermediary, Nookomis?" Gidjie asks. She's grown up learning standards about life from Intermediaries. She's been told that humans are more vulnerable to the affects time has on things, but everything seems blurred when she tries to understand what it means that she's human and they're not.

Soon enough, I won't have my best friend. And I'm not going to live as long as anyone else in my family? Why am I a human? What am I supposed to do? Gidjie thinks on the subject, having only a moment to concern before Nookomis answers her question.

"Well, I reckon it is, being how I'm here now, normal as I'll ever get," her hands on her hips.

Gidjie and Carver look to Bluebelle, who is losing her liveliness with each moment. They know what happens next in the rising process.

"Should we head up?" Gidjie asks him, looking down from her roost on the bench to meet his attention.

"She's right you know, things are meant to change," he looks serious, and then says, "but some things don't!" and in an instant he's in opossum form and running towards the closet, where his not-so-proper escape route is.

"Hey!" Gidjie laughs, knowing exactly where he's headed. She runs past him and closes the closet door. He grunts, running head-first into it.

"See, what'd I tell ya! Some things never change!" he yells out into the hallway after her, rubbing the top of his head. He turns back into his human self to reach the doorknob before beginning his opossum shimmy up the crack in the stone.

"Don't forget to flip the sign!" Nookomis hollers at the both of them.

Gidjie runs into the lift down the hall and begins stepping up and down on the press plate in the corner that makes it go up. To go down, you use the plate in the opposite corner. Rumor has it—rumored by her aunts—that if you step on both plates at just the right time, the lift will divert to a secret room.

Gidjie and Carver have tested this, to Nookomis' annoyance, who would be left waiting to use the lift for nearly an hour while they played. They have yet to cause the lift to stop anywhere but along its normal, vertical path within the five stories of the dwelling.

Going down beneath ground level, the stories are as follows: floor 1 is the sanctuary; floor 2, the living quarters; floor 3, the baking floor; and floor 4 is the Ancient Traders Market.

The lift makes it up to the very top floor, the sanctuary, and then one more, to the one and only Above World level: The Animals-R-A-Wares shop, which sits on top of them all like an umbrella, Gidjie likes to think. The shop is also the only place in the residence where she gets to interact with other humans.

Dancing with anticipation, her foot comes to a stop on the push plate as the door slides open. She peers around the dark, early morning atmosphere of the shop. It's completely quiet.

"Beat ya!" Carver's voice rings down from the top of the lift as she takes her first step out.

"Cheater!" Gidjie squeals in surprise, turning to watch the lift slowly lower itself down to align perfectly with the rest of the floor, leaving no sign of a lift at all, just a beaming opossum Carver in a 'ta-dah' pose in the middle of the shop.

"Cheater has to unlock the gate," she lifts her eyebrows up and down, motioning out through the covered window nearby a couple of times, "Besides, Nookomis said you're supposed to use proper doors, so your mom doesn't..."

"Fine," he says, walking towards the front door of the shop. He pushes his opossum self through the small animal door built into it, and then re-enters after a moment and says, "Oops, forgot. Let me try that again." A second later, he is grinning humanly at her.

He unlocks and walks through the door like an average human, then down to the gate at the end of the driveway. He waves back at her, a dopey grin on his face, making sure she sees him doing everything as a human would. He knows Nookomis expects her human customers to not be scared off by wild, roaming, albeit adorable opossums.

"You forgot to flip the sign!" she yells as he's nearly halfway back up the driveway.

Animals-R-A-Wares

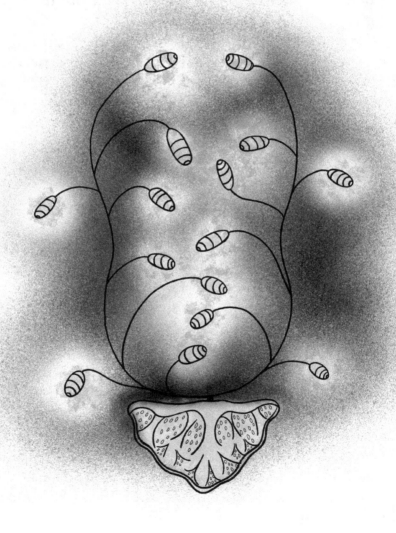

"Can you tidy up on that side, and I'll work over here today?" Gidjie asks, physically blocking Carver, who's got a hungry look in his eye and is galloping in her direction. She points with her lips and tilts her chin up at the opposite side of the shop.

"Really?" he asks, "Again?"

"Did you forget what happened last time I let you *help* over here during fizzlit season?"

He peers around the front, and then back of her, to gaze longingly to where the plump, purple fizzlit berries that come once a year are kept.

She leans back to meet his gaze, "We had to spend the better half of a week accounting for and paying back the..."

He sighs, "I know, I know. You're right. They're just soooo good."

"That's why I'm looking out for you and letting you work elsewhere, so you're not fighting the urge to dive in head-first. Again." In an attempt to cheer him up, she adds, "They'll be done for the season soon, only a few more days to go," she reassures him.

Fizzlit berries come from a place Gidjie has never been and only heard little about. They grow underground in small quantities, high along the walls of the Confluence—a place where traveling barterers, storytellers, and hands-for-hire set up camp along their routes. It's also where the Elder Councils meet.

Now, you're probably wondering how berry bushes are able to grow underground. Thanks to a supply of ecosystem-supporting gasses—similar in importance to those pumped out of hydrothermal vents deep in the ocean, where no sunlight reaches—life in the Confluence

41

thrives. And there are many similar places within the Earth where unique life forms flourish.

Gidjie's been told that on occasion, the mixture of gases in the Confluence is such that they could have an unpredictable effect on her physiology. It's one of the reasons few humans have ever set foot there over the millennia. It's typically forbidden.

Getting back to the fizzlit berries. To acquire them, you either have to be a fizzlit fruit bat, or be in good standing with the Fizzlit Harvester Society—a society of bats that collects and decides how to distribute the fruit. It so happens that Nookomis is in very high standing, on account of helping them recover from an awful case of blighted berry bushes.

As the story goes, a sleepwalking fungal mass had wandered into the cave and bedded down in the soil behind where fizzlit plants were growing. As he dreamt, he exuded a substance, that while comforted him, was toxic to the berries, causing them to rot.

After an investigation, Nookomis found and woke him up. He was disoriented, apologetic, and required help finding his way home.

The circular Animals-R-A-Wares shop is made of stone from floor to ceiling, including the rows that extend inward from the edges toward the center. To the untrained eye, the rows appear to be solid structures.

However, if you know where to stand and how to look, you might glimpse one of the many hidden openings along the stone cupboard spaces.

The interior of the rows is hollow and full of ramps, stairs, storage units and pulley devices, just the right size for the various providers of goods—Intermediaries and full-time animals alike. At any given moment, a parade of tiny purveyors is streaming in from the Above World, as well as the depths below.

Carver begins moping towards his designated work area for the day, until he sees the family of skunks piling out of the stone wall and forming a line to the bin where they store their goods.

The first, and largest skunk, carries a birch bark basket full of insects. He pours them out and quickly covers the bin while the others scramble to pick up stray, fleeing insects. They pass them from one skunk to the next, before the first in line places the miniature, skunk-deemed-goodies into the bin. A few crunches can be heard as the littlest in line decides the insects are easier to eat than wrangle.

Bugs have the tendency to wander off, so there are always little skunk hands reaching out from behind the wall to get them back into their bin.

Humans never want them, although kids get excited, screech, and do an 'Oh my god, it's BUGS!' dance when they see them. Occasionally, they'll catch a glimpse of a furry hand or a striped tail, but their parents always chalk it up to an overactive imagination.

Now don't think that because humans aren't enthusiastic about insects, that they're not highly sought after by a large portion of the animal kingdom.

Some insects are eaten, yes. But *all* insects are keepers of secrets, big and small. Think of the one secret you wish you could know; there is an insect out there that knows it.

After-hours and occasionally between human visits, other kinds of patrons visit the Animals-R-A-Wares shop. The insect bin is always one of the firsts to empty.

It helps that the skunks themselves are the friendliest you will ever meet. If you've never met a skunk, you should know that trouble tends to avoid them, thanks to their inborn, musky deterrent. This allows them the liberty to be cheery and high-spirited most of the time.

Carver is in an instant his opossum-self, rushing to help the skunks set things in order. Opossum Carver loves insects; human Carver, not as much. Gidjie has seen him eat a beetle on more than one occasion in human form, however.

"Carver!" Gidjie bellows, eyes wide, stomping her foot.

"Shoot. Forgot again," he says, resuming human form and squatting down low to continue his assistance.

What's going on with him today? He's usually not so forgetful, she thinks, borderline worried.

Gidjie gets close enough to peer over his shoulder and checks the bin like she does every morning, wondering if it's possible that Intermediary insects exist. She's heard stories of them getting so caught up in life as a particular animal, that they forget they have the ability to assume a human form. She'd feel terrible if one came through the shop unnoticed as a tiny bug.

"Do you think Nookomis is getting forgetful?" she asks him after examining the bin.

"What do you mean?" he says, sitting on his haunches, holding up a caterpillar that's perched on the tip of his finger.

"Nookomis said Bluebelle's been in the family 100 years, but that she met her for the first time 150 years ago. It doesn't make sense. She's either forgetful or she's keeping secrets from us."

"Like what?"

"I don't know, like…about *time travel*." She feels embarrassed the instant it slips out of her mouth. *Time travel? Ha!* She begins standing up so she can scurry off and hide on the other side of the shop.

"A relative said a strange thing to my mom once that I've never understood," he starts, "It was on her birthday. You know how she says she's the same age every year? Well one year, after she announced she was turning 36 again, my uncle said, 'maybe if you played the melody stones *backwards*, you could make it an *official* 36!' I've never seen my mom so mad. That was 5 years ago. He's still not allowed at our house."

"Did you ask her what your uncle meant by it?"

Carver raises an eyebrow at Gidjie, "You're joking, right? Didn't I just say she got madder than I've ever seen her?"

She shrugs, "Yeah, I guess I like having you around."

"Ha. Ha. You'd be lost without me, kid," he says, before erupting into real laughter.

Satisfied with his attentiveness to the skunks, Gidjie heads over to the wall behind the counter at the back of the shop and heaves mightily upon an old hand crank in a clockwise direction.

Stone slabs retreat down the walls, revealing glass windows and a sunny spring morning. Just to the right of the crank is a 'Do Not Open' sign hanging on a cabinet at eye level. She dusts it off before opening it, "Good morning!" she exclaims happily.

Behind this particular cabinet door, lies a busy world of ant, bee, and wasp purveyors.

Now, these are full-time insects, but unlike the ones hunted down by the skunks—a hunt that is based on an ancient pact between skunk and insect—they are here to stock their own goods in the rows of shelves lining the wall behind the counter.

Gidjie's noticed that insects from certain colonies seem to have a collective consciousness; that is, their behaviors are concerted, and their presence is that of one organism. She often wonders how large such an organism could be—how far down underfoot and wide across the world can one extend?

In any case, they bring in a dazzling assortment of things: cultivated fungi; a variety of honeys people fill recycled jars with—or in Carver's case, his mouth; as well as wasp-made papers that have fascinating properties. One of Gidjie's favorite foods is made by ants, deep in their underground chambers: cheeses made from wild nuts, seeds, flowers, and just about every other wild delicious thing you can imagine.

The ants that roll the cheese wheels up the many tiny ramps from way down and out of sight are brownish-red and shiny. The cheesemakers themselves, are tiny and covered with a colorful, squishy, crumbly, fuzzy coating. These smaller ants only come up every so often, to inspect the cheese in the shop for freshness.

Gidjie and her grandmother provide some of the items in the shop. You'd be surprised how many fascinating and nutritious cooking ingredients you can gather from a rocky cliff, or a tall, gangly tree, if you have the advantage of flight, as Nookomis does.

The two have developed an arrangement that works for them. Several times a week, Nookomis goes out to gather while Gidjie awaits her harvest. It's up to Gidjie to create recipes in the kitchen with the ingredients, decide how to best present them in the shop, and explain what they are and make suggestions on how to prepare them to curious patrons.

Because of this arrangement, Gidjie has become the main cook of the house. She's always eager to try the many ingredients that come into the Animals-R-A-Wares shop from all over. She also has a fairly wide knowledge of Above World wild foods that she knows how to identify and harvest herself.

Twice, however, she has accidently made a sleeping potion of a meal that sent her and Nookomis to sleep for a week.

Each time she awoke, Carver was waiting by her bedside. All Gidjie could remember about what had happened right before the slumber, was that a hooded, amphibious merchant had delivered little roots by way of the middle door, a day before she had made each sleepy meal.

The third time the amphibian had returned, Gidjie remembered him and what the roots were responsible for.

She labeled the jar clearly, and rather than place it in the kitchen of their living quarters, she put it in a special collection of items in a pantry on the baking floor.

The
Tourist
and
the
Turtle

"This place is paradise!" the human in the khaki colored hat with a dangling rope under his chin says to Gidjie. He winks at her, his cheeks a little weighted from age but creamy and showing no sign of bug bites, yet.

By the end of the weekend, he'll be full of bites and stories about giant mosquitos and armies of wood ticks and … Gidjie thinks.

"You've got it made, kid," he adds, giving a second wink.

She *hates* it when people wink at her; she never knows how to interpret a wink.

Carver snickers as he tends a shelf nearby.

"If you love it, why don't you move here?" Gidjie asks.

He gives a pause and then, "Nah, as much as I love the peace and quiet of the North Shore, the missus and I need our movie theaters and take-out food; and good beer of course!" He looks around and then shakes his head, "I'd go nuts with nothing to do for too long."

Nothing to do? Gidjie reiterates the statement internally. Her mind leaves the conversation. Her head begins to spin, thinking about what might happen if people who bore easily were to move to the area. She envisions parking lots and gas stations taking over the forest, the shoreline littered with trash.

Am I really human? she puzzles, confused for the umpteenth time by the dramatic conflict of interests she has with most humans she meets.

Nookomis is standing beside her, and notices her face turning pale. She gently grabs the items Gidjie was about to pack, and places them safely in a bag for the man.

"Thank you, ma'am," he says, "How much do I owe ya?"

53

Had Gidjie not spaced out, she would be excited in this moment, for her favorite part of working in the shop, is the bridge-building between animal and human needs. It's in these moments she truly feels a part of Intermediary culture.

"Let's see. One bottle of sunscreen and two wild herbal teas will be…" Nookomis looks down at the piece of paper in her hand, "well, I'll let you have a look at the numbers. My eyes aren't what they used to be," she says, handing the man the piece of paper.

He scratches the side of his head, pushing the cotton hat off-kilter as he reads the receipt in disbelief.

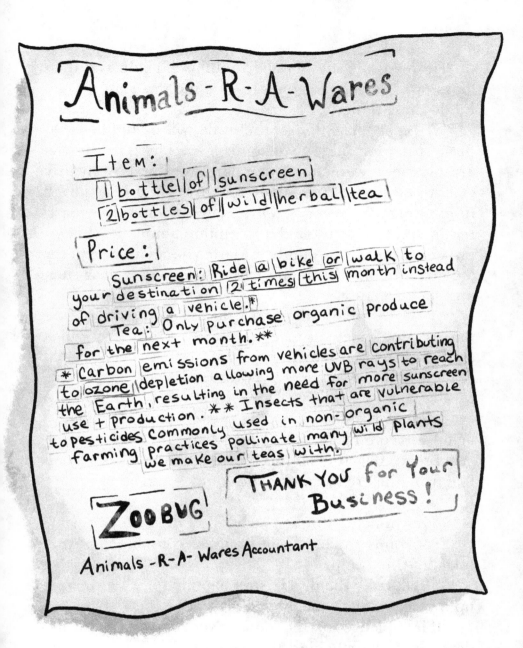

Animals-R-A-Wares

Item:
1 bottle of sunscreen
2 bottles of wild herbal tea

Price:
Sunscreen: Ride a bike or walk to your destination 2 times this month instead of driving a vehicle.*
Tea: Only purchase organic produce for the next month.**

* Carbon emissions from vehicles are contributing to ozone depletion allowing more UVB rays to reach the Earth, resulting in the need for more sunscreen use + production. ** Insects that are vulnerable to pesticides commonly used in non-organic farming practices pollinate many wild plants we make our teas with.

ZOOBUG

THANK YOU for your Business!

Animals-R-A-Wares Accountant

"Is this a joke?" the man says, confounded, "…ride a bike and only purchase organic produce for a month?"

He reads the slip of paper to himself again and then looks up, "So, you're going to give me this stuff if I say I'll do these things?"

"*If you do* those things, the trade will be fulfilled. Do the terms seem fair?" Nookomis asks. The terms of the arrangement were fairly standard, seeing how nearly everything in the Animals-R-A-Wares shop is acquired in exchange for pledges. Oftentimes, trading for goods require pledges to rebuild or maintain animal habitats.

For instance, certain bees barter honey in return for a pledge to 'plant so many native wildflowers near such and such location.'

"Well, I suppose they do," he shakes his head, "the missus is never going to believe this." He does a quick scan of his environment for indication of where he'd really wandered into, "I've never heard of anything like this."

Nookomis smiles, nodding politely at him, "Thanks again for coming in. Oh, I forgot the bread. Everyone gets bread. Baked fresh this morning." She takes a small loaf from the bread rack on the counter and adds it to his things.

"How much—I mean—what do I do for the bread?"

Nookomis smiles, "The bread is complimentary. A token of friendship."

"Well, okay then!" He says happily, picking the bag up. He leaves the shop, chuckling in disbelief.

"First pledge of the day," Nookomis says, sitting down in a chair behind the counter to talk to Zoobug, the shop's accountant, "and we'll be seeing more tourists every day now for the next few months—you better get your inkpads ready," she says, teasingly.

As far as Gidjie can tell, Zoobug is both plant and animal—and then some—all in one.

During business hours, Zoobug sits in a pot under the countertop, creating receipts just out of sight from customers. She has extensive knowledge on all matters of trade, and Gidjie suspects that Zoobug may understand every language on the planet.

Between customers, she can be found listening intently to the needs of the shop's merchants, who pay her visits one by one.

Understanding Zoobug is another story, for she makes clicks and vibrations that Gidjie has mostly yet to decipher, apart from the basics like 'water' and 'thanks.' Nookomis, on the other hand, is stellar at interpreting Zoobug's every sound and gesture, and brings her almost everywhere she goes, after business hours. As far as Gidjie is concerned, Zoobug is her grandmother's best friend.

Animals-R-A-Wares only accepts the invention of human currency, by way of the donation jar Nookomis *had* to put on the counter—for safety reasons. A customer once got so angry that their money wasn't valued, that they threw it at Gidjie and stormed out of the shop yelling profanities. So now, if a customer gets excited in a not-so-good way about the trade-and-pledge system, Nookomis gives a nod to the jar, and that's where they put the money.

However, just because humans insist on putting money in the donation jar and walking out with an item from the shop, that doesn't mean they're off the hook for any ignored terms of the trade. Gidjie and Nookomis won't stop them from leaving, but an entire branch of Intermediary culture is built to *encourage* accountability.

Zoobug creates copies of every transaction using wasp paper and smart-spore ink, and places them in a cedar box under the counter. When pledges are carried out satisfactorily, they simply decompose, leaving tiny mushrooms from which spores are harvested for making more ink.

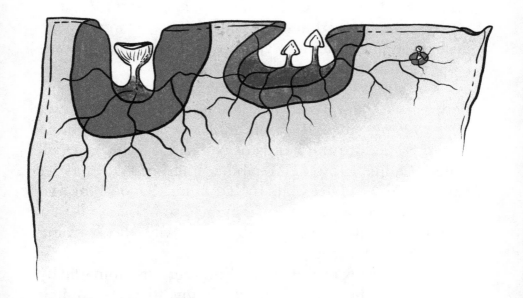

However, if pledges are neglected, those receipts remain intact and are collected at the beginning of the next lunar month by an Enforcer.

The means by which Enforcers procure results are little different today than those used by the first Intermediaries to hold the position.

Enforcers are like trickster bounty hunters, and are occasionally behind things that gremlins, ghouls, ghosts, curses or the like are said to be responsible for.

Each enforcer has a particular way they go about their enforcing—like a calling card, if you will.

Gidjie's grandparents were Enforcers back in the day, until they ended up with a handful of Anishinaabe kids they rescued from a burned down boarding school. Gidjie's parents were among those who had no homes to return to, and so Nookomis and her husband started a learning camp of their own.

However, after a couple of years, they were met with opposition from one of the elder councils, and the camp was disbanded. By that time, Gidjie's parents were of age and chose to continue to camp with other young adults from the boarding school.

The disbanding of the school caused a disturbance between Nookomis and her husband, and they haven't lived together since. It wasn't until years later that Gidjie would come into the hands of Nookomis. These are all things Gidjie knows little about but has had a brief rundown of over the years by her aunts. Beyond this, no one will tell her what really happened to her parents, her grandfather, the other children, or why the learning camp was disbanded.

Getting back to Enforcers. Enforcers are nomadic by trade, and although retired, Nookomis still gets the itch to travel on occasion. Once or twice a year, they drive around in an old school bus giving educational tours.

The tour-bus-with-a-twist, as Gidjie likes to call it, relies on the concerted efforts of Intermediaries and animals to teach bus riders things about local natural and human history. It's not quite the same as enforcing, but the humans getting on the bus have no idea what they're in for. They leave the experience with a shift in their thinking, regarding the role humans play on the landscape. And that's always fun to see.

As the man in the hat begins backing down the driveway, "Ow!" Carver yelps from just out of sight.

"Are you okay?" Gidjie stumbles out of her stupor and walks hurriedly towards him.

"Yeah. Agongos got me again is all," he says, "I took an acorn to the eye this time."

She rounds the corner to where Carver is and can't help but laugh. He's standing with one palm over his right eye, looking up at a high shelf where a tiny chipmunk is sitting, his cheeks stuffed with acorns.

"I was trying to pick up one of his acorns, after it fell onto a lower shelf, but he beat me to it, turned around and kicked it at me, and it hit me in the eye. Then he ran down here, picked it up, scampered back up to his bin, and now he's grinning at me with it in his cheek!"

Carver's still looking up angrily at Agongos, the chipmunk. He turns to Gidjie, who's covering a snicker. He realizes how ridiculous it must seem and begins to laugh, "Do you ever think he'll get the hang of store *and* trade? How will he trade them, if he can't handle anyone even touching one?"

"Well, he's got the storing part down at least," Gidjie says, laughing, "his acorn bin's always full."

Just then, a snake courier enters the shop on a message track that runs along the floor behind the counter. It pushes the wooden beads strung along the track to spell out the code for 'check road.'

"Oh no, not again," Gidjie frets.

"A box, Gidjie," Nookomis directs her.

She hurries to the storage closet and finds a box that is small-animal-sized.

The three of them run down the driveway to the main road. Sure enough, there is a turtle on its back near the ditch.

Nookomis kneels down and gently turns her over to see an inch-long shell crack, "We've seen worse," she says.

Nookomis is right, but it's bad enough that it makes Gidjie sad, and then angry. She turns towards the SUV in the distance. The man and his missus make their way unknowingly toward their vacation spot further up the lake. She roars out loud towards them, like a tiger might, she imagines.

Carver sees her in action and thinks she looks more like a tiger cub than a tigress. Even so, she's scary enough for him to not point it out.

The turtle is having trouble moving her leg closest to the crack, "The box, Gidjie" Nookomis says, motioning to her.

Gidjie hands her the box, dropping to her knee, "How's she doing?"

"We'll get her to the sanctuary, and I'll have a better look at her," Nookomis says, lifting the turtle gently into the box. She hands her to Gidjie, before picking herself up and brushing little pebbles from her knees.

Carver looks into the box and shakes his head, "You're gonna be okay, friend," he tells the turtle.

The Sanctuary

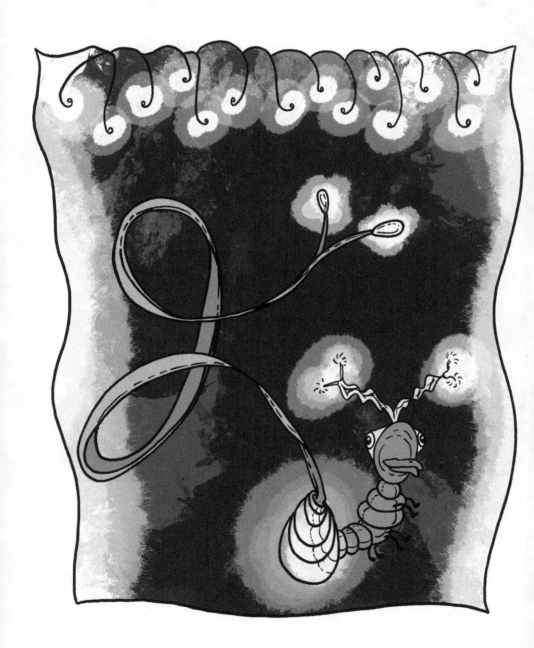

Luminescent glowworms, twinkling like stars of various colors and sizes, hang from the ceiling of the sanctuary that encompasses the entirety of the first floor down. Lightening lichens line the walls, helping to illuminate an ecosystem that functions to heal transitory visitors.

Thanks to a Lighting Expert that comes by to care for the living light fixtures on a regular basis, the lichen are able to create two types of light: soft glowing ripples of color, similar to the aurora borealis at night, and a steady white-ish light, like that of natural sunlight. Lightening lichen light is known to have a soothing effect on anyone who might find themselves in the sanctuary. In addition to the glowworms and lichens, there are a variety of bioluminescent fungi and animals as well.

The sanctuary receives fresh water that's fed by an underground river. A small waterfall cascades in on one side and flows through the level, feeding calm pools sustaining diverse life, before exiting through a tunnel on the other side.

There are many hidden entrances to the sanctuary from the Above World. Some are big enough for a mouse, while others can accommodate a rabbit, a coyote, and so on.

Occasionally, an animal comes here for medical treatment and remains in the refuge of the sanctuary and patrolled forested grounds surrounding the Animals-R-A-Wares shop for many years. Most who find themselves here, however, heal expeditiously and are soon able to return to life in the wild.

In addition to those in recovery, there are sanctuary helpers. The helpers tend to those who are healing, as well as accommodate the service providers that come on a need-basis.

The beavers, for example, come about once a week to service the underground river, making sure it's in good working order. They pat down soil, level out uneven places in the ground and remove any clogs in the tunnels they find.

The animals and Intermediaries that are currently in the sanctuary are on the mend from the likes of: accidents with cars; flying into windows; deliberate attempts by humans to harm or kill them; and a few are survivors of other animals attacking them during a hunt.

The type of wound an animal has, determines the type of medicine they require, as well as the medicines they *create* in their own bloodstream as they heal.

The medicines animals create themselves, are then passed along in the bloodstream to any offspring they have. These medicines are like stories of survival, passed down to make the next generation more resilient.

Gidjie and Carver leave Nookomis to assess the turtle's condition, and retreat to the place in the sanctuary they go to in just this kind of situation.

Unlike a waiting room at a human hospital, theirs isn't sterile and uncomfortable. Instead, it's full of healing bacteria, plants and animals, and comes equipped with two hammocks and a fruit basket.

"Are they really coming this time?" Carver asks from inside the basket, the lid bouncing atop his opossum head while he rummages through the fruit Nookomis keeps in it just for him.

"Why, so you can tell Flaurinzia you love her again?" Gidjie says from her hammock, tilting her head to see if there's any visible response from him.

The lid stops moving. She knew her comment might embarrass him a little, but he also knew she would bring it up. He's never been bashful about his crush, and Gidjie agrees with him, her aunt *is* pretty amazing, so she doesn't tease him *too* much.

Flaurinzia is smart and witty and loves to laugh and is always quick to play with them, in whatever game they wish her to join. And she always tells the most fantastical stories about the island where she lives and works.

Gidjie flops off of her hammock, and walks over to the basket. She gives it a little nudge with her stockinged foot to prompt a response from him.

"She's really not all *that* great," he says, which is immediately followed by an audible 'gulp'.

Gidjie gasps dramatically and pulls the lid off to look at him as she doesn't believe him, "Tell me one person, one, who is lovelier than my aunt."

He looks embarrassed he'd said anything. He shakes his head and plops firmly down on his behind, crossing his arms. "Hmph," he says, "wouldn't you like to know. Maybe if you hadn't kicked my basket and made me drop my berries, I'd tell you." He's looking away from her now.

"I'm sorry, Carver," Gidjie says, realizing she's being pushy on a subject that doesn't really matter. It's just been an endearing charm of his, talking about her aunt in an admiring way; but this year, he's been different. Maybe he doesn't think her aunt's all that great anymore. Or, maybe he doesn't want to talk about such things openly with her. Whatever it is, she decides to drop the subject.

She digs into a dress pocket, "Here," she says, pulling her hand out and reaching down low into the basket in front of his arms, which were crossed in protest.

Incapable of being controlled, his nose starts to sniff. Realizing what she's holding, he turns to snatch them up, quickly shoving the whole pile of tiny strawberries into his mouth with both hands, "Thunnnkss!" he says, his juicy lips spraying his thank you all over her hand.

"Nookomis and I went out picking yesterday," she says, pulling her hand out of the basket and wiping it on her dress.

He looks up, casting a hurt look at her, his cheeks still bulging, "And you didn't come get me?"

"You know how your mom's been lately. Besides, Nookomis said you'd eat all of them before we could even get them into your basket," she teases, giving the top of his furry head a brisk rub. He pulls away from her and she realizes he doesn't like that anymore either.

Gidjie stands up, and wonders for the very first time if it is weird to pet your friend. Apparently, it's weird now. She decides to leave it at that and give Carver the personal space he needs. She places the top on the basket, but he pushes it up under the weight of her hand.

"I'm coming out," he says, vacating the basket, the tip of his long, thin tail the last thing to exit.

"Got any more of those strawberries?" he asks, hands on his belly, eyes beaming.

Gidjie smiles, "For you, I've got maybe 5 or 6," she says, knowing very well that they put away quite a few more than that with his name on them.

Carver is in an instant a boy.

Gidjie bursts out laughing, "Carver, your face is covered in juice."

He scrubs at his cheeks roughly with both hands, "Better?"

She studies his face for a moment then abruptly turns away from him and scrambles back onto the hammock. She closes her eyes, "Yep, all good," she says. "They're in the cooling room on the third floor, you know where."

He walks past her with a look of 'what'd I do?' on his face, before going off to find the strawberries.

Whiskers

"Gidjie, our turtle friend requires 3 short calls on a snapjaw," Nookomis says, waking her up from her nap, "Please fill this jar up, that should do the trick," she hands her a small glass jar with a lid. Gidjie puts it into her shoulder bag.

"Is she going to be okay?" Gidjie concerns, rubbing her eyes.

"I believe so, but we need the short calls, Gidjie, the short calls, please my girl," Nookomis motions her up out of the hammock.

Gidjie looks around but doesn't see Carver.

"He went home," Nookomis says, "his mother sent for him."

Gidjie notices the basket is moving. She lifts the lid. It's Carver's little raccoon cousin, Acey, who is helping himself to some fruit, "Hey Acey," she greets him.

"Hi Gidjie!" he says, waving a sticky paw at her.

She puts the lid back on and walks to where small harvesting baskets hang nearby.

"Be mindful of Whiskers; I saw her outside a bit ago," Nookomis informs Gidjie.

"I will," Gidjie says, stepping onto the lift.

"Take your asemaa,* my girl," Nookomis reminds her.

Gidjie stops on the second floor where their sleeping quarters are, and grabs her little asemaa pouch off of the table near the entrance to the lift. She tucks it into a pocket, before getting back on the lift and heading up to the Animals-R-A-Wares shop level.

---

*Asemaa is traditional 'tobacco.' Although Nookomis is not Anishinaabe and doesn't use asemaa herself (she uses certain powdered minerals as offerings), she encourages Gidjie to do so.

Gidjie exits the lift and notices that the shop is looking tidy. The merchants are good at maintaining their individual shop nooks and helping each other out as needed.

It's been a short day for human business, because of the turtle incident, and the merchants are now getting their wares in proper shape for the night barter, which occurs every night between all beings except humans.

She flips the sign in the window from OPEN to CLOSED and walks over to the hand crank behind the counter. She hefts on it in a counter-clockwise direction, raising the stone slabs to cover the windows. The glowing light fixtures along the walls come on. They will illuminate the shop until the slabs are again lowered.

Gidjie exits the shop and walks into the late afternoon sun, in search of turtle medicine she's never gathered before.

"The way I see it, if I'm bringing a foreign predator into a community of creatures who might be alarmed to see this predator near their homes and families, it is my responsibility to alert the community of the presence. I wouldn't set a lion loose in the Midwestern scrublands and expect zero grief, would I?"

Gidjie looks down at the black, fluffy cat, who had met her just outside the shop door and now walks beside her. The fluff ball looks up happily at Gidjie with bright yellow eyes, before trotting quickly ahead of her towards the start of the forest path.

Gidjie sounds a crow-style alarm call for 'cat.'

Whiskers hunkers down low. She turns around, giving Gidjie a look as if to say she was spoiling her fun. She slinks back and plops down at Gidjie's feet.

Gidjie digs in her shoulder bag, making sure she has the jar for harvesting the 3 short calls on a snapjaw.

"Well, Whiskers, what do you expect? You are a cat. What was I supposed to say? I'm not about to be responsible for your thievery of fledglings or young chipmunks. Not after what happened last time," Gidjie looks down at the aloof creature, who is rolling around on her back.

Last time, Whiskers hadn't only killed a nest full of robin chicks but didn't even eat a single one. The robin parents had visited Zoobug the next day and Whiskers wasn't seen for a little while after that. Gidjie never knew what had happened exactly, but figured Whiskers must've had to deal with the grievances of the robin parents, in one-way or another.

Whiskers shoots Gidjie a look of half shame, half, 'what do you expect, like you said, I'm a cat.'

"Fair enough," Gidjie tells her, "as long as we do our best to keep a balance, that's what matters."

They make their way to the entrance of the path. The little chickadees that had been hopping around on the lower branches of a white cedar tree, were now up high, with all eyes on Whiskers.

Gidjie loves the cedar and spruce trees here. They're big enough that she can walk upright under the lowest branches without ruffling her hair, and the forest floor is soft with moss and evergreen needles from the pines.

Whiskers runs fast ahead when she sees her favorite scratching tree, just inside the start of the trail. She gives a long stretch up it, accentuating every one of her hairs as she makes her display of claw-sharpening approval. She turns to Gidjie when she's finished, requesting a scratch on her head to verify Gidjie did indeed see her display, and is welcoming of her on her walk, despite their differences.

"We're looking for 3 short calls on a snapjaw," she tells Whiskers, acknowledging her with a head scritch, "I don't suppose you've seen any snapjaws recently?"

Whiskers purrs loud, lifting her haunches high under the scritch of Gidjie's fingernails.

"The only snapjaw I know, is old Akiiwi. Last time I saw her, she was at the river near the bend."

The bend in the river where the local snapjaw likes to hang out, happens to be near where the closest human neighbors—Whiskers' humans—like to go trout fishing in the summertime.

"Well..." Gidjie says, "I don't think it's trout season yet, so we should be okay." She looks down at Whiskers, "What am I saying? It's not like *you* have any reason to avoid them."

What Gidjie knows about the neighbors, is that they've lived in the house a mile down the road for about 5 years. There's Whiskers, a mother, a father, and two boys; one just older than Gidjie, and the other, several years younger. She's only interacted with them in the shop a couple of times. The first time they came to check out the place, was shortly after they moved in. They've only been back one time since, and that was because there was too much snow for them to make it to one of the towns along the North Shore for supplies.

The only other time Gidjie has had interactions with the family, is when the father and eldest boy were out fishing a couple of years ago.

In addition to the fact that Gidjie is afraid of unpredictable human behavior, she also typically has a hard time holding conversation with strangers, without becoming anxious and uncomfortable. Add on top of that, the fact that when she usually runs into strangers by herself, it's in the middle of the woods, making whoever it is she runs into, extra curious and questioning of her being there. This leads to more anxiety, as her explanations regarding what she's doing, usually results in a blank stare by the humans, followed by more questions.

What would *you* say to a girl you run into out in the woods when she tells you she's gathering 3 short calls on a snapjaw to help heal a turtle?

Akiiwi and the Chickadee

"C'mon, Whiskers," Gidjie tells her trail companion, "there's a turtle counting on us today."

On their way through the forest, Gidjie takes notice of the plant distribution and phenology. The pine trees become interspersed with aspen, oak and cherry, before giving way to a scrubland of hazelnut, wild rose, and blooming raspberry bushes. Soon the white blooms will fall, and the ends of twigs will swell into hard, green fruit, that plump up red in the hot summer sun.

She sighs, deeply in love with the procession of life.

They reach the line of alders, growing near the water's edge, where the river is deep and cool.

Gidjie crouches down, cupping her hands to gather up a palm-sized body of water, mirroring her reflection, "Do you think my mom and dad looked anything like me?" she asks Whiskers, who stops lapping water nearby to give her hands a nudge with her head, causing a little of the water to spill.

She lowers her hands. The water, now full of her wondering, is released back to the river. Her question about her parents, carried downstream.

As her focus sinks below the surface of the river, she notices another pair of eyes looking back at her, besides her own. They are red and black striped, and unblinking. She gasps and stumbles back on her heels, falling atop Whiskers, who scurries off.

"Akiiwi!" she exclaims in a whisper.

She digs a pinch of asemaa out of her pouch and holds it closed in her palm. She closes her eyes. She lets herself feel everything that's happened so far in the day, and then focuses in on the need of the turtle.

"Gichi-manidoo, manidoo ziibi, Akiiwi, Gijigijigaaneshiinh indizhinikaaz," she says, identifying herself to the spirit of mystery, the river, and the snap jaw. She informs all why she is there; that a turtle is in need of medicine. She asks for pity and for help. She thanks them for their listening, and then opens her eyes.

She releases the asemaa onto the surface of the water, then takes several steps back and turns to scramble up a small incline. She finds an inviting spot by a bush, and sits, just out of view of the shoreline.

The minutes go by, and she remains with an open heart and mind, listening in to life around and within her.

Just as she is getting stiff in the legs and starts to shift around, she hears it: the skin-tingling sound of water rushing off of an enormous shell, as the ancient turtle makes her way out of the river and onto the shore.

Gidjie can hear feet padding slowly, and the sound of shell dragging across earth and pebble, as Akiiwi presses up the incline.

The hair on Gidjie's arms is standing on end. Akiiwi is still out of sight. She closes her eyes and waits until the sounds are quieted down, before slowly opening them.

The air in her lungs becomes trapped for a moment. Akiiwi is staring into her eyes, inches from her face.

Their heads are about the same size, and all Gidjie can see are Akiiwi's eyes. Everything else in the world blurs.

Until…

Chirp-chirp-chirp.
Chirp-chirp-chirp.
Chirp-chirp-chirp.

A tiny, black-capped chickadee is hopping up the back of the snapjaw in Gidjie's peripheral, making its way onto the turtle's enormous head.

Slowly, she brings her gaze from Akiiwi's stare, to see the chickadee is holding a clump of lichen in its beak. It tilts its head to one side and then the other, and when it's satisfied that Gidjie has gotten a good look, it flies away.

Akiiwi breaks her gaze upon Gidjie and begins making her way back down towards the river.

Gidjie's breath returns, and she realizes she needs to act quickly. She fumbles for the glass jar and crawls on her hands and knees behind the retreating Akiiwi, searching the tiny ecosystem of lichens, mosses, slime molds and tiny plants upon her back, for the particular medicine she had been shown.

She fills the jar and replaces it in her bag. Before she gets up, she acknowledges those who had heard and responded to her for their help, including gijigijigaaneshiinh, the chickadee.

Gidjie's namesake is the chickadee, and it was now clear to Gidjie why Nookomis had sent her out to gather the 3 short calls; she knew the little bird could help Gidjie find what was needed.

"Come on, let's get back to the sanctuary," she tells Whiskers, who had stayed hidden in a nearby bush to watch the action.

Whiskers comes out stretching, and the two make their way home, Gidjie recognizing that her fear of the bend in the river had morphed into a feeling of empowerment and trust.

The Aunties

Gidjie exits the lift at the sanctuary. She finds her grandmother digging seeds and bits of eaten fruit out of Carver's basket, surely the aftermath of Acey. Nookomis tosses a few dried plums into it when she's finished.

"Here you are, Nookomis," Gidjie says, handing her the little jar containing the 3 short calls.

Nookomis beams, "Thank you my girl," she says, before going off to tend to the turtle.

"Ew, a human."

Gidjie turns to see Molandoras, who's wearing a half grin. She notices the flash of her aunt's blue hair that's mixed with greys, and the fact that she's using a cane on the left side, before Molandoras can drop down to her wolf form.

Despite having the use of just three of her legs, Molandoras quickly circles Gidjie to give her a playful bite on the back of the knee.

"Ah!" Gidjie exclaims, trying to pull her leg free from her aunt's toothy grip.

She knows Molandoras doesn't mean anything by the comment '*Ew, a human.*' At least not when it's directed at *her*.

Molandoras has always been the easiest to upset when it comes to humans, and she's never been afraid to voice it. Directly to them. In the shop. With little or no provocation from the humans on the receiving end of her scowling.

Molandoras' tactics for dealing with humans clashes with Nookomis'.

Nookomis stands firm in her assertion that Intermediaries ought to help humans find balance with the earth and other living beings, rather than chide them for not knowing or remembering how. She says that because humans are social beings, they are prone to being forgetful, as many things can disrupt the fluidity of human memory from one generation to the next: natural catastrophe, wide-spread disease, genocide, the forced removal from homelands, and so on.

Anyways, with Molandoras spending most of her time in the boundary waters area, researching a family of full-time wolves and the effects that hunting has on the wolf family structure, there's been a less confrontational atmosphere around the shop.

"Auntie!" Gidjie squeals in delight after several moments of hopping around and crouches down to embrace her aunt's wolfly affections head-on.

"Gidjie!" she hears, while being ambushed with a hug around the neck from behind.

She turns to see her younger aunt, "Flaurinzia! You both made it!" she exclaims, "It's been way too long since you were both home last," she hugs Flaurinzia tightly.

"Yeah, you'd think one aunt who lives not all that far from here, *should* be able to make it home at least as often as another who lives way out in the middle of the ocean," Flaurinzia says, literally poking at her sister.

Molandoras snaps her jaws at her sister's finger, playfully but with attitude.

"How's life on the island?" Gidjie asks Flaurinzia.

"It's life as usual," she squeezes Gidjie's shoulder affectionately, and adds, "I brought you something."

Gidjie jumps up and does a dance of excitement.

When it comes to far-out-there jobs in the realm of Intermediary work, Flaurinzia's is literally far out.

Her council is stationed on an island, where she helps watch over a colony of birds that live in the inner rim of a volcano.

What kind of bird, you may ask, lives in a volcano? The kind that no human scientist has ever plucked a feather from or scribbled in a notebook about the likes of. And there are more kinds like that than one might think.

Most of Flaurinzia's time on the island, is spent as a gliding cliff mouse, nestling amongst the eggs and soft, downy-feathered chicks of the Silvertip Weavers—as her aunt calls the birds. She watches over the younglings and helps protect them from the occasional giant cat that ventures too far from the forest below.

The giant cats on the island are also unknown to modern cladistics, and like the Silvertip Weavers, are watched over by members of Flaurinzia's council. An interesting thing about these cats, is that they're herbivores.

Even so, the Silvertip nests must be guarded, for the cats have been known to squeeze amongst them to nap, resulting in the inadvertent falling of chicks into the perilous depths of the volcano.

What's especially peculiar, is that the birds are always welcoming of the cats, even though they cause so much accidental damage to the colony.

Gidjie's never seen the island, the birds, or the cats, but she's spent a good amount of time daydreaming about them.

One of the most interesting things Gidjie's learned about the Silvertips, is that they have hands for feet.

They weave their hanging basket nests with the tentacles of giant squids. They catch the squids in the ocean and hang the tentacles to cure in the gasses of the volcano, as deep down along the edge as they possibly can without burning up.

The special gasses found in this particular island's volcano, not only dry the tentacles, but bind with them so as to create super-strong, stretchy, cord-like material that has a perpetual warming quality to it.

The birds use the hanging baskets for sleeping, storing crabs, and an array of random things they find in the ocean.

Flaurinzia says that the Silvertips learned to weave from an ancient society that once lived in the oceans. They were the original caretakers of the island, but they haven't been seen or heard from in a long time. The main essence of the work that Flaurinzia's council is responsible for, is solving the mystery of where these caretakers have gone, and helping maintain a balance on the island until they return.

Flaurinzia has brought back all kinds of interesting things that the birds have gathered over the years. Most of what she brings home during visits, end up in the Ancient Traders Market on the fourth floor.

Occasionally, she brings a special item meant for Gidjie.

She sits down, and pats the ground next to her, motioning Gidjie to join her, "Last month, I had a dream about you, and that same week, I found this," Flaurinzia's extra-wide smile is enough to make Gidjie anxious, "My dream told me it's meant to be in your company."

She pulls a blue velvet sack gently from her shoulder bag, and from the sack, takes out a hand-sized wad of black fabric. She carefully unwraps it.

"Is that a…seed?" Gidjie inquires.

"Yes, it is," Flaurinzia beams.

Molandoras is sitting next to them, an admirable and scrutinizing grey wolf. She leans in, giving the giant seed a sniff. In an instant, she is her human form, her eyes wide, jaw dropped. She looks to her sister, "*Where* did you find *that*?"

"Never mind this—where did *you* get *that*?" Flaurinzia returns the question to Molandoras, who was absent-mindedly rubbing an exposed and very badly bruised left ankle.

Molandoras pulls her pant leg down to cover her injury and shoots her sister a painful look, "Not everything in life is ocean paradise and treasure."

She resumes her wolfly configuration, and gruffly trots away with as little limp as she can manage, to where Nookomis is caring for the turtle.

"She thinks she can hide things from me, but she can't," Flaurinzia says, squinting towards her sister. She returns her gaze to Gidjie, and her expression softens, "Here," she says, "this is your responsibility now."

Flaurinzia places the black fabric and seed into Gidjie's hands.

"It's warm," Gidjie says, surprised.

"Keep it in this," Flaurinzia says, handing her the blue velvet sack, which is also warm.

Gidjie peers into it, "This is a Silvertip bag," she tells her aunt.

"Yes, it is."

"And it's been beautifully stitched with velvet," Gidjie's says, admiring it. She's never seen one like it.

"Keep the seed under your bed, Gidjie," Flaurinzia tells her, "Sleep with it near."

Gidjie admires the goose-egg-sized seed. It's multi-colored, with little vein patterns running across it. Looking at it for more than a moment, she thinks she sees the veins throb.

"You'll know what to do when the time comes," Flaurinzia says, smiling big before getting up to follow after her sister.

Gidjie remains in a seated ponder, looking down at the seed, "Do? Do what?"

The Miigwech'n Kitchen

The Miigwech'n Kitchen, the 'Thankful Kitchen,' as Gidjie refers to it, is a mobile, café-esque medic tent, that her, Nookomis, and occasionally Carver employ. Its purpose is to allow for the comfortable care and release of animals and Intermediaries that are almost ready to leave the sanctuary. It also serves to help those need of spontaneous care.

Currently, it's erected in a meadow, edged by a grove made entirely of a single aspen organism.

Bejeweled-green, wavering arms of trees, connected by an ancient root system far more sophisticated than one could ever imagine, reach out towards the tent, as if to pull them near and offer comfort.

One thing about this kitchen, is that you never know who'll be coming for dinner.

The evening is setting in and condensation is gathering on the outside of the tent. A few dew drops run down the lifted door flap into the entrance of the main room.

"Eight, nine, ten," Gidjie counts them from her cot.

You can tell a colder night is coming, by how much water is squeezed out of the air at the end of the day. Some nights, there are no drops this early—it's barely dusk. Gidjie knows that tonight will be on the chillier side.

She walks over to the opposite side of the front room and collects a small log, placing it on the fire before climbing back onto her cot.

Her sleeping quarters are nestled near the door, away from the kitchen portion of the tent in the back. She can see part of Nookomis' cooking fire through a crack in the fabric wall at the head of her cot.

Gidjie has access to the living space at the front of the tent, as well as the door; but after-dark-exit is forbidden without Nookomis' permission.

During the day, she helps set up the tent, bring in water, firewood, and tend to patients. She also assists Nookomis with herbs and equipment. However, after dusk, the kitchen portion of the tent in the back is off-limits.

Another glistening dew drop starts its journey falling free through space. It is absorbed mid-descent by a form in the darkness of the doorway.

She squints past the flames of the fire, trying to make out what's there. The figure shifts, and Gidjie recognizes makwa, a bear.

"Please, come in," Nookomis says kindly, from behind the wall in the kitchen.

Gidjie can see her through the crack. She is standing behind a large pot, that sits cooling atop a rock the size of an ironing board.

Makwa looks at Gidjie but says nothing as she walks in quietly towards an opening in the fabric wall that's being held by Nookomis.

Gidjie lies on her cot for the next hour, trying to listen in on what's going on behind the wall. All she can hear are tongue clicks, low grunting, air blowing and teeth clacking from the bear, and an occasional inaudible word from Nookomis.

Gidjie is nearly asleep when she hears through the veil of a starting dream, what is undoubtedly a bear's voice:

...Molandoras...wolves...missing...

Soon after, she is fast asleep, forgetting all about the bear, and unaware that Nookomis is slipping out of the tent and off into the eventide.

Just before dawn, Gidjie wakes to a rustling in the tree line nearby. She sleepily flops out of her cot and stumbles to the door, which is closed, and without thinking pulls the canvas flap up, looking out into the retreating darkness of a newly budding day.

A very large, brilliant red fox with extra-ordinarily long black legs—unlike any fox she has ever seen—is walking with much character along the edge of the wood line about forty feet away.

His long, sleek, black nose tips slightly downwards, needling the air, threading the rest of his body behind him through the forest.

The fox sees her looking at him, and he switches direction—towards her—quickening his pace.

"EEP!" Gidjie yelps, turning away from him, desperately fumbling for the rope to tie the flap back onto its holding rod beside the door.

Before she can get the flap closed, the red fox is in the doorway, standing up on his hind legs.

He's as tall as an adult human. She couldn't see any movement within him when he was walking along the brush line, nor does she now. He's not an Intermediary.

How is he standing up? A full-time fox? Is it too dark to see any movement? she wonders, but the fire is still aglow in the center of the tent and the daylight is brightening with each moment. There's plenty of light to see.

The fox pushes his way into the tent. He stands before her and stares steadily into her eyes and says, "Dance with me, will you?"

"Huh?" Gidjie returns, bewildered.

The fox reaches a paw into a red, furry pack at his waist and produces a stringed instrument the size of a small plate. It's round and layered like a tiered cake, with strings strung from one level to the next.

With the instrument in hand, the fox initiates a magnetizing, mesmerizing melody. And then, he begins to yip and sing:

> *Dance with me* YIP! *in this way*
> *I need your help my friend* YIP! YIP!
> *My children have all gone off to play* YIP!
> *And I cannot find them* YIP! YIP! YIP!

The giant red fox is hopping in a clockwise circle in the middle of the tent next to the fire.

Come on YIP!
Dance with me YIP! YIP! YIP! YIP!

The fox's song is far too inviting for Gidjie to not join in. She begins to hop up and down in a clockwise manner, holding her arms up like a fox pup might.

He resumes playing the instrument. Gidjie has the sensation that the music is being played on her very own heart strings. That she is being *taught* how to play this song and dance this dance with her heart.

After a minute or two of this, the door flap of the tent lifts up one, two, three times, as three fox pups come hopping in to join the dance, each different than the last. In fact, Gidjie isn't sure if they actually are all fox pups, but they are dancing and singing like one family unit.

Filled with such an intense feeling of familial love, and coupled with the spinning, she becomes dizzy. She lies down on her cot and hugs herself, closing her eyes.

She falls back asleep, and the earth of foxes dance their way out of the tent, and into the dawn of the forest.

You Accepted

A couple hours later, Gidjie wakes with the dream on her mind. She sits up fast. *Had* it been a dream? She leaps from her cot and begins searching the tent for signs of dancing foxes. The door is tied shut and Nookomis is asleep on her own cot closer to the door.

She walks to the central fire, now a low glow of embers. She closes her eyes, the music alive inside her.

She begins to hop.

Around and around she hops until she hears Nookomis' voice, "What are you doing up so early? And, hopping? You'll give yourself a sick stomach before breakfast."

Gidjie sees Nookomis is smiling when she opens her eyes, obviously curious about her behavior. She goes to her grandmother and sits down beside her and tells her all about the foxes, the familial bond she felt between them, the music that tied it all together and how she can still feel all of it living inside of her.

Nookomis listens attentively, and at the end she is quiet, a serious look on her face, "My girl, this is very surprising."

"What do you mean?" Gidjie is caught off guard by the tone in Nookomis' voice.

"Last night you were asked for help *in this tent*...and you accepted?"

"I danced, if that's what you mean," Gidjie says, confused about what it meant to her grandmother, "Wasn't it just a dream?"

"I say not. Rather, I believe you were invited to help solve a very real problem that's happening even as we speak," she says, "and you accepted."

"But..." Gidjie starts, "I don't understand what you're talking about."

"You know how your aunts have councils of peers that they work with, solving problems by utilizing their individual gifts?"

"Yes," Gidjie answers slowly, her heart beginning to race.

"What you experienced last night is what I would consider a formal invitation to seek *your* council," Nookomis is leaned in close enough that her breath is kissing Gidjie's face. Her dark, glistening eyes piercing intensely into Gidjie's, "and, you accepted."

After spending the last few years preparing herself for the very opposite of this to happen, the idea seems less than believable, "No. No, no, no, no, no," Gidjie retreats to her own cot and plops down, holding the sides of her head in her hands. Her eyes blinking large, "But I'm a *human*," she insists, looking at Nookomis, pleadingly, "Why would the fox come to this tent? And ask *me*?"

"Gidjie, this is a medicine tent. All who are inside and capable of answering a call for help must oblige, within their capabilities," Nookomis pauses a moment and walks over to sit down beside her, gently placing a hand on her knee, "The manner in which the foxes appeared to you, tells me that you have been gifted a bond of trust and responsibility."

"What does that mean?"

"Well, at times they will help you when you are in need of guidance. And when you are asked to help them, you will be there. This is how the rite to council is initiated. It's different for everyone, but the essence of the bonding is always the same. You'll find that the bond extends beyond foxes. It is our duty, as those who have a foot in both the Above and Between Worlds, to make good on our responsibility to do what we can to help bridge the communication gap between the humans and the animals. It is an honor to uphold this responsibility."

Gidjie can't help but feel afraid and caught off guard. She had resolved that she'd never join a council, because she is human, not Intermediary, "But what if bad things happen to me? What if humans *get* me?"

"Humans aren't going to get you, Gidjie, if you remember what I have taught you, you will go unseen by any humans that might want to cause ill will to a young woman."

Gidjie touches the stone hanging around her neck. She knows she is to only flip the stone from white to black in certain circumstances. It has a magnetic pull to it that keeps it in place on her chest. She's never taken it off and doesn't remember ever not having it. She's never flipped it, and isn't really sure what would happen if she ever needed to.

"Can you… come with me?" Gidjie ventures.

"You know I can't. It's tradition that the youth go alone."

"You're really not reacting how I'd expect you too, Nookomis."

"I admit, I'm a little concerned, but I am mostly happy for you. You get to start a council. *A human girl.* On a council. In this day and age," Nookomis says, beaming with pride, then suddenly shifts to concern, "Your guide will get you to the Great Beaver Pole Lodge. That is where all young councils in our area meet for the first time. It's tradition."

"My guide?"

"The lodge is more than a day's walk from here. I insist you employ the service of a guide, if you are to get to the lodge in a timely fashion. You'll leave first thing in the morning."

The fear of the unknown begins to rise under Gidjie's skin. She can sense that there are unsettling matters unfolding and that *she* is meant to address them. The awfulness of the feeling is enough to balance out the amount of joy and love she carries from the fox dance.

In a strange new way, she feels calm and balanced, "Carver's never going to believe this." Her stomach sinks. She'd be leaving Carver behind.

"I don't mean to upset you, but more than you know might be counting on your journey being successful, as is usually the case. But don't worry; I know who we can rely on to get you to council. And he is the best guide there is."

Mino, Stone, and the Floating Island

"A firefly?" Gidjie asks aloud, squinting towards a blinking light approaching from a ways down the tunnel. It seems to have stopped moving.

The door creaks open behind her, "Put this in your bag, Gidjie." Nookomis hands her a cloth sack from the *inside* of the middle door.

Gidjie has never been more exhilarated and terrified in her life. She is on the *other* side of the middle door. About to set off into an unknown she's only dreamed of.

Now, however, peering out into the darkness, the unknown seems kind of like the middle of nowhere—or everywhere, perhaps, depending on how you look at things.

The sack smells of bread and dried snacks—smells that are recognizable and comforting. The tunnels, on the other hand, are full of new and curious aromas.

Gidjie doesn't look at what's in the sack, as she nervously fumbles to place it alongside her asemaa, water bottle, and a few other small items in her shoulder bag, "It's so dark."

"For now. Light comes and goes around here," Nookomis smiles, clearly amused with the amount of newness one small step into the Between World has brought her granddaughter, "Do you have the seed?"

"Yup," Gidjie says, patting her bag gently, watching as the light resumes getting bigger, brighter, closer.

Her mouth drops open when she sees what the light is sitting on.

It's a toad. A full-time toad. On two legs. Gidjie squints, trying harder to make out any sign of movement within the toad. There's none.

The toad is about as tall as Gidjie's knee and is holding the source of light above his head as he walks closer to her.

"Legend has it, your granddad dug these tunnels, long time ago," a voice says from the darkness near the toad, which Gidjie can now see is actually standing still; it is the ground underneath the toad that is moving.

The toad is riding an island.

"What the?" Gidjie baffles.

"It's time I leave you, my girl, you're in good hands," Nookomis says.

"You'll tell Carver where I am and what happened?"

"I will," Nookomis agrees. He hadn't shown up the night before and wasn't at home when Gidjie had gone to look for him before heading down to the tunnels to wait for her guide.

"What's my guide's name again?" she asks in a whisper.

"Mino."

"Mino," Gidjie says aloud, "Mino, Mino, Mino."

"That would be me," says the voice, now just five arm lengths away.

"Hey, I know you!" Gidjie says, happy to see a familiar face, "You're the Delivery Service...person."

"Delivery Agent, and you can now call me by my name," he says, still smiling and giving a wave of his hand to let Gidjie know she should come aboard.

"Mino? Am I saying it right?" she asks, stepping onto the island, which on closer inspection is maybe twenty feet across and covered with sand and plant life. The length is hidden in shadow, as it's too long to be fully illuminated by the toad's light, "Like, a minnow?"

"That's me," the tiny man says.

"Your companion looks like a toad."

Mino gives her a look like, 'what'd you expect?' and says, "He *is* kind of a toad."

"A kind of toad, or kind of a toad?"

Mino shrugs.

The toad places the lightning bug onto a post in the middle of the island and then plops down onto his haunches.

"Let's not go getting too comfortable yet, Stone" Mino tells him.

"Did you call him 'Stone'?" Gidjie asks.

"Well it's his name, isn't it?" Mino says, giving her a small side-eye.

"So...Mino and Stone."

"Uh huh," he says, one eyebrow raised in suspicion of further questioning, "but I have other names."

"Like?"

"Like, N-guh!" Mino starts and then stops abruptly while making an unintelligent sound as one might when caught off guard. His shoulders are scrunched up to his head. He looks embarrassed, like he didn't mean to say anything.

"N-guh?" Gidjie asks, genuinely unsure if that is in fact another one of his names or not.

"Oh, you know," he starts, trying to sound cool, "Flies by Fish," he says, giving a head nod in the direction of a few fish with what look like saddles and other equipment she's unfamiliar with attached to them. Their reigns are loosely tied to a small post on the inside edge of a tiny inlet. One of them wriggles about, and a flitter catches the light. The fish has wings.

He then kicks a tiny pebble and turns to muffle over his shoulder in a cough, "Pond Scum."

"Pond Scum?" Gidjie turns to him, "Why would anyone call you such a thing?"

"Well maybe I've been known to eat an algae sandwich or two, okay?"

Gidjie laughs, "Well, I'm sure it's delicious," she says, pretty sure that it *could* be delicious, but had never had one.

"Oh, they're the best!" Mino says, "I'll make you one sometime," the tiny man beams, "It's a secret family recipe."

"It's awful that 'scum' is in the name though," Gidjie thinks for a moment, "What about Pond Grazer? Or Pond Chow? Or Algae Wrangler?" Gidjie laughs, seeing the serious look of consideration on his face.

"Pond Grazer," he repeats out loud, "I like it." He turns to Stone, "Let's get these young ones to council, shall we?"

The toad remains seated. He begins to squish wet sand in his toes while gesturing Gidjie's way and to the darkness behind her. He crosses his arms over his chest, plops onto his back, spreads his legs out wide and immediately begins to snore.

Is he faking? Gidjie wonders.

"Stone?" Mino says.

One of the toad's eyelids open and then shuts quickly, after seeing Mino looking directly at him.

Definitely faking.

Eyes still shut, Stone drops a hand down from his belly to point a finger to the side of where Gidjie is standing.

"Stone, we don't have time for this. Oh! before I forget, I better drop off this package for Grandmother Blue Jay. Said her ears could use a pair of these," he hops down off of the island and places a wrapped package beside the middle door.

"Grandmother Blue Jay?" Gidjie says aloud, as she's never heard anyone refer to Nookomis in such a way.

A movement in her shoulder bag distracts her from the thought. She digs around it and is about to resign herself to believe she had imagined it, when she finds the jar. The lid is off, and the dough isn't inside.

"What the?" she begins to frantically dig through the items. She gets to the bottom, where the seed is tucked securely in the Silvertip bag.

Without looking, she slips her hand inside. She can feel the seed is nice and warm and—*what's this?* There's something tacky-feeling stuck to it. She peers down into the bag and sees the dough is stuck to the side of the seed. She tries to peel it off, but it is stickily attached. Gidjie blinks her eyes stupidly, and then goes in for a closer inspection. The veins of the seed appear to be extending into the dough.

Just then, she is pulled aside by a pair of hands as Mino and Stone continue with their dysfunctional but altogether hilarious conversation.

"Gidjie, I have to tell you something."

She jerks her hand out of the bag and turns startled to meet the eyes of Carver, who is stepping out of the darkness behind her.

Missing

"Gidjie…" he says, holding up his hand to stop her before she can say anything. He knows that what he needs to tell her is not going to be easy to hear, which is why he had been pacing the shadows of the island trying to think of a way to tell her, "your aunt Molandoras and the wolf pack she was studying are missing."

Gidjie's excitement is burst abruptly, "What? What do you mean missing?"

"A snake visited me two nights ago," he starts, and then stops to read her expression to see if she knows what he means by this. He can see that she does, so he continues, "I've been terrified to tell anyone I was invited to council. You know how my mom is."

Gidjie's face sinks a little at the fact that he hadn't told her, even though she had been away, camped out in the Miigwech'n Kitchen with Nookomis for the last three nights.

"I thought I was gonna have to sneak off to council without telling her, but then it just blurted out of my mouth this morning when I overheard Nookomis talking about Molandoras and *your* invitation to council. Mom was upset with me, of course, for talking to the snake, and for accepting the call that was offered," he says. "Our council *has* to be connected to Molandoras' disappearance."

Our council? Gidjie thinks, caught off guard by this crazy notion; a notion that only days ago she would have laughed at herself for even considering possible. *Of course* they are to be in the same council, if they are called so closely in time. But she had never in a million years thought she would receive that call. She always thought Carver would leave home one day and she'd hardly see him after that.

Gidjie's heart begins beating fast; she can't believe she had forgotten what makwa had said that night in the tent. She'd fallen asleep and it had gotten lost in her dreaming.

"Why wouldn't Nookomis tell me any of this?" she says, feeling a little ambushed. She never thought she would get a call to council, or that it could be so heart-wrenching.

"All I know, is she helped convinced my mom it was best for me to go. And I'm really, really glad you're here," he says, looking genuinely relieved. The tone in his voice shifts and his next words come out more slowly, "That's not all. This last year I've had several offers to form council, but I couldn't..."

"You've been acting like nothing's been going on this *whole time*! I mean, sure you've been goofier and more forgetful than normal, but..." she sighs. Now's not the time to be mad at him. Molandoras is missing. And they're both here, now. "I've been worried about you. But now, Molandoras," her eyes water up, "she could be in trouble with...humans."

"Yes," Carver says, "she could be," and then adds, "but the fact that a council has been called in this matter means she must still be okay."

The two walk over to where a fire is burning near the front of the island, which was now traveling back in the direction it had come from, to the north.

They sit looking out into the tunnels ahead, the island moving into complete darkness. How Mino is able to see to steer properly, Gidjie is unaware, but the island seems to move intuitively.

118

The sound of water rushing against the little island making its way through the tunnels, carrying them to council, is a sound Gidjie will never forget.

They sit quietly with their thoughts for what seems like hours. After a while, Gidjie begins to feel worn out from all of the excitement and upset of the last two days, "I'm tired," she says.

"Get comfortable," Carver says, "I'll tell you a story."

Gidjie lies down near the fire, her head resting on her shoulder bag. She watches as the glowing lights of bioluminescent creatures appear and disappear along the walls of the tunnel. A rush of wind flows through from the distance.

She looks over to the lightning bug that Stone had placed on a little post near the center of the island. The lightning bug is also getting comfortable for the night, lying on its side with its head propped up on one of its bumpy legs.

"My mother says your grandfather was a great peacemaker. One time, he wrestled an entire clan of alligators that was holding a community of water mammals hostage.

"The smaller mammals were being bullied harshly; the alligators were refusing to leave until one of the mammals could beat one of the alligators at wrestling.

"The mammals were to choose their most promising wrestler at the start of each day; the alligators did the same.

"Each day, the mammal population diminished, as each day, the chosen was eaten.

"Your grandfather heard about the bullying and set off to tunneling right away. He was a fast digger and thought that arriving from below would give him an element of surprise.

"He was so driven to help the poor community of water mammals and not let one more of them be eaten, that he had tunneled his way to the swamps of what is now called Florida in just one night.

"His tunnel ended where the bottom of the swamp began.

"At the bottom, he found the skin of the losing competitor from the day before and tied it around his face.

"He emerged from the water to sit among the other mammals, and soon volunteered to be the next competitor.

"The alligators saw he was bigger than the other mammals, but being boastful, declared he would make a fine meal, being larger in size as he was.

"When he beat the first alligator, the others were so angry that they rushed at him, determined to not let a lowly water mammal get an upper hand.

"One by one, he beat those gators."

They pass by a very old sign that reads 'To Florida,' with an arrow pointing in the opposite direction to where they're headed.

The sign looks as if there had been other things written on it over the years, with 'To Florida' being the newest designation of place names.

Carver points to it, "This is that tunnel," he says.

Gidjie can hardly believe all of this. The fox, Molandoras, Carver, her grandfather's tale.

Her eyes feel heavy. It's not long before they are closed tight, and she is off to sleep.

The Great Beaver Pole Lodge

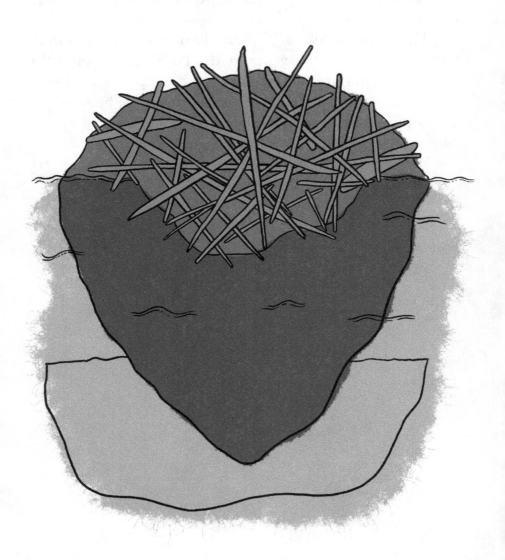

"I bet they're way cooler than me, and smarter, and funnier, and…" *oh no, not the slug feeling again*, Gidjie thinks. Her body slows down, her head droops backwards, her mouth falls open. She doesn't want to go on.

Carver, who was just in the lead, circles around to the side of her and uses his forearm to guide her gently forward. He knows if she stops moving altogether, it will be hard to get her moving forward again—like it was the last two times she did this since they stepped off of the island and were bid good luck by Mino and Stone an hour ago.

Moving forward, very slowly, Gidjie scrunches up her face, deep in thought about how to get out of meeting the other members of their council.

"Just a human here," she laughs nervously, talking to herself, "going off to form a council. Nothing odd or frightening about that."

Carver knows she's afraid of what the other council members will think when they find out there's a human among them, and has been doing his best to reassure her, "If they really are as cool as you're imagining, then they're going to love you."

It was then that Gidjie realized they had made their way up to a warm, earthen-smelling room. A fire burns low in a clay oven ahead. A vent that is full of a web-like material hangs over the hearth.

"It looks like the smoke's being filtered," Carver says, after following Gidjie's gaze, "Makes sense, can't have humans seeing smoke coming out of a beaver lodge."

His comment about humans makes her weak in the knees, but she nods in agreement.

She looks down to her feet. Beneath them are smooth river stones and moss.

Gidjie and Carver do a slow turn, taking in their environment. There are water holes polka-dotting the floor of the room.

"Underwater entries?" Carver supposes.

There is a splash of water behind them.

"Checking in?" a beaver asks them, as he slides up out of one of the water holes on his belly, affirming Carver's guess.

Gidjie sees movement within the beaver and knows this is an Intermediary they are dealing with.

"Hi, yes," Carver tells him.

"New council, I take it, eh?" the beaver says, his tiny eyes bulging with both glee and gravity as large as they can possibly widen.

"That's right," Carver says.

"The rest of your council is here already. I can show you the way," he says, standing upright on two legs and trotting quickly past them towards an upward-leading hallway covered in bright white clay.

In fact, apart from the entry room, everywhere else in the Great Beaver Pole Lodge is smoothed over with clay.

There are various shades of reds, browns and black, mixed to create elaborate patterns. Decorative stones and pieces of wood are pressed into the walls here and there.

They try to keep up with the beaver, who's smaller than they are, but who's hind legs are moving rather quickly for their size. His flat beaver tail swishes back and forth behind him, sending Carver hopping backwards to avoid being smacked in the ankles.

The hallway is like a large, upward-leading spiral. They pass at least a dozen rooms. There are doorways that are tiny and stacked on top of each other, with little ramps winding up the wall to reach them. Other doorways are large. Regardless of size, all have a glistening, lightweight fabric hanging in front of them, making it impossible to see in from the hallway.

"Here you are, young council members," the beaver says, drawing the cloth aside for them.

"Oh shoot, oh shoot, oh shoot, oh shoot," Gidjie whispers, her heart once again beating fast as she and Carver enter into a smaller hallway. The beaver lowers the fabric door.

Candles dot the walls in recesses, illuminating the hall brightly. There are three doorways on each side, each covered with the same fabric.

"Six rooms," Carver says aloud, obviously curious as to how many members are in their council.

"This is incredible," Gidjie says, letting out her held breath to allow for amazement to take hold.

"Isn't it?" Carver says, smiling at the fact that they were here. Together. Moving forward.

"Wait, I hear voices," Gidjie says.

"Everyone else must be here already," Carver says, walking forward. Gidjie grabs the arm of his shirt, and he stops to listen with her.

There is a bend in the hallway ahead, and as they make their way slowly towards it, they can hear voices.

"Zhee, cut it out, I'm trying to concentrate!"

Gidjie looks at Carver and whispers, "Two of them?"

"I can't help it, I told ja! Don't choo think if I could help it, I would...help it?"

The two voices burst out into laughter.

"Both of you need to remember what we're doing here and quit yelling; it's not very respectful," a third voice says.

"Three?" Carver raises an eyebrow.

They creep closer.

There is a brief pause in the conversation of the voices, followed by an eruption of laughter from everyone out of sight. They are still laughing as Carver and Gidjie reach a sheer, shimmering curtain. Carver pulls it back before Gidjie can stop him.

There are three kids sitting in an earthen circle in the middle of a black, round, dome-topped room that has a starry sky design formed into it, flowing around the curvature of the room.

"Whoa," Gidjie says, "it's like the sky," she points with her lips, uplifting her chin towards the wall to the left, "It's the River of Souls, the Milky Way," she says, tracing the sky map across the room until she runs into three sets of unblinking eyes.

They are all staring at her.

"N-guh!" Gidjie buffoons, a choked gulp of air escaping her mouth unintelligently.

With that, the room is again filled with laughter.

A Council is Born

"I'm Carver," he says, moving in quickly to shake a hand of each of the kids.

Gidjie doesn't hear them introduce themselves, as her ears are pounding loudly in embarrassment.

When Carver has shaken each hand, the four of them look to Gidjie. She takes a deep breath and approaches the circle.

She nods and shakes the closest hand, "Hi, I'm Gidjie," she says, more coolly than she thought possible.

"Nice to meet you, Gidjie, I'm Onie," the girl with reddish brown hair and deep green eyes says, as she turns into a young deer, still shaking Gidjie's hand.

Okay, she seems pretty nice, Gidjie thinks. She pulls away her hand, which is sticky with nervous sweat and wipes it across her dress.

She turns to the next kid in the circle, a boy with thick, black eyebrows and shoulder-length black hair. And his feet. They are duck feet. They are the only part on him that isn't in human form.

That's odd, Gidjie thinks, *I've never seen that before.*

The boy shakes Gidjie's hand, and noticing she is staring at his feet, he says, "I usually wear moccasins, but I thought in the name of the occasion, I'd go tradish today." Everyone except Gidjie laughs.

Gidjie knows this to mean he is 'going traditional.' Even *more* traditional than moccasins. *So* traditional, in fact, that he wasn't wearing *any* shoes. Just his duck feet.

"I'm Gidjie," she says, and can't help but erupt into laughter when he begins wiggling his ducky toes for emphasis.

"I'm Zhee," he says.

The next boy in line is in his animal form, but Gidjie's not entirely sure what he is. She finds this odd, seeing as

131

how she's seen nearly every type of animal around for at least a hundred miles.

"I'm Roze," the mystery animal introduces himself first, seeing she has a puzzled look on her face rather than a hello for him.

"I'm Gidjie," she says, shaking his hand slowly and turning her head this way and that, trying to get a better look at his markings, "Are you a kind of bear?" she asks, genuinely stumped.

Onie, Zhee, and Roze laugh.

"He's kind of like a bear," Onie says, "but in a small package."

"I'll…bite you!" the small, bear-like person tells her, trying to keep a straight face while showing his teeth.

"Wolverines are ruthless, I hear," the duck-boy chimes in, laughing himself over, his webbed feet flying straight up into the air.

Ah. A wolverine, Gidjie thinks. *That makes sense.* She's heard of them but had never seen one.

Gidjie and Carver look at each other. They are now officially part of the group; they have been addressed by all. It's time to join the circle.

In an instant, Carver is his opossum self, plopping down happily to fit into an empty spot next to Zhee.

"Cool," Onie says, "we have an opossum."

The circle widens to accommodate Gidjie, as she wedges herself—her very humanly self—between Carver and Onie. She fidgets with her bag, avoiding the looks from the other members, who are obviously curious what form—and therefore what gift—she brings to the council.

Should I tell them about Molandoras? She wonders. *When is a good time to tell them I'm human?* Is her next thought. *Never, that's when.*

"Now that we're all here, it's time we take ourselves seriously," Zhee says, in a nasally voice.

They all look over at him and burst out laughing. Only his head looks like a duck. The rest of him is regular, kid-sized, making the small duck head look tiny.

"I'm hungry," Roze says, rubbing his growling stomach. He lies down on his belly with his arms stretched in front of him. His legs bounce up and down, his fluffy tail wiggles behind him, his chin rests on the ground.

He plays with a bug, letting it climb up and down and up over each of his claws on its march through their council chambers.

Gidjie, Zhee, Carver and Onie all begin to laugh. None of them have a wolverine in the family and so find the sight of him amusing.

"What?" Roze says, looking at them from one to the next, before looking at himself and realizing what they must be laughing at, "Well, get used to it!" he says, rolling over on his back and wriggling in the cool, soft soil. He makes a couple of happy wolverine grunts, and everyone laughs harder.

Zhee is in an instant a full-bodied duck, and with a couple of flaps, he is across the circle and on top of Roze. The two wrestle around for a few minutes; Gidjie, Carver, and Onie laughing harder than they've ever laughed before at the sight of them.

When they've picked themselves up off of their sides and brushed the dirt off, "Hey, I have snacks," Gidjie says, taking out the sack of food and passing it first to Roze, who takes a piece of bread from it and then passes it around the circle.

"I'm glad I'm a duck," Zhee says, "We get to fly away and go where the food is." He thinks a little bit, "But we're still not safe from hunters. Have you all heard about human whistles?"

Everyone looks stumped.

"They're like duck whistles, but they sound like humans. We employ squirrels to use them during certain times of the year, to help lure human hunters away from where we like to eat."

"Wow, I've never heard that before," Carver says, "I guess I've never really known any ducks, personally. Until now," he can't help but grin at Zhee.

"We live in Canada. Our family is huge, and we all live in different parts of a deep, old den that spreads out under land that is covered in snow much of the year," Roze says, "Everyone in my family is a wolverine. And those of us who aren't born wolverine, are buried in a birthing den, in a special place in the North," he says, "Once you're in there, they bury you, and you have to dig your way out to reach the Above World. By the time you reach the top, you've crawled through all kinds of wolverine medicine; through rivers of wolverine dreams that flow heavy in the soil. When you get to the top, you've been re-born wolverine, and are expected to keep that form," Roze's face turns solemn, "Like my cousin, who was born a bobcat. He made a good bobcat. He was happier a bobcat. But he's forbidden to *be* a bobcat. It's just not done in our family."

Quiet expressions of empathy are exchanged.

"We live on the outskirts of Duluth in a human-made house. My mom is a private investigator for humans, but she never lets me help her. I spend most of my time researching paranormal activity on the internet. I keep a journal about activity in the Great Lakes Region. Oftentimes, it's the work of Enforcers. But not all of the time."

"What exactly *is* the internet?" Gidjie asks her, unashamedly. She's watched people stare into their phones, and has heard mention of the internet before, but has never asked anyone for a tutorial. She's never felt the need to. Phones and computers are things they've never needed in their house.

"It's how humans communicate with each other from all over the world," Onie says.

Gidjie hesitates but for a moment, and then tells them the story about how her parents were rescued from the boarding school and adopted by her Intermediary grandparents.

She sits nervously looking around at the other council members, wondering if they realize what the part about her parents being rescued from a human boarding school meant.

Onie is the first, and only one who catches on, "You're...human?"

Gidjie puckers her lips and jaw up tight, closes her eyes and slowly nods her head 'yes'.

Gasps from Zhee and Roze.

Gidjie opens her eyes. They're all staring at her, including Carver, who's giving her a look like, 'say something.'

"I'm Anishinaabe," she sighs, "but I don't know what my parents were like." Being raised by Nookomis and her aunts, Gidjie's never felt that she's missed out on a family. But there's something about being in this safe space that's allowing feelings of sadness to arise in her. "I mean, sometimes a human identifying as Anishinaabe, or Ojibwe, will come into the shop to trade wild rice for things. Some of them teach me things about being Anishinaabe, and they tell me stories. I like when they come in. It makes me feel closer to my parents."

"I've known her all my life; best human there ever was, practically an Intermediary herself, apart from, you know, not having an animal form," Carver says, turning back into his human form, and looking a bit defensive.

"How were you invited to council?" Roze asks her, neverminding Carver's interjection.

Gidjie tells them about the night the fox had visited her and asked her to dance.

"A fox came to me, too!" Zhee says, "Dang near frightened my mom to death! A big ole' fox, just yippin and yappin around, frolickin all over where we nested down for the night. He even stepped on my aunt's foot!" He laughs, "I'm sure she's not going to let me forget about that anytime soon."

They take turns recounting stories of how they received an invitation to council: both Gidjie and Zhee were visited by foxes; wolves appeared to Onie and Roze; and a snake found its way to Carver.

"So, you're a human. Is there anything you can do?" Roze continues his questioning.

"What kind of question is that? She can do lots of things," Carver says, still sounding over-protective.

"I can cook, and I know about all kinds of foods. We get things in the shop from all over," Gidjie says. She thinks hard before saying, "I know what it's like to be human living in an Intermediary family. And I can always tell an Intermediary when I see one. And I have this necklace," she says, touching the stone, "But, I'm not sure what it does. I'm only supposed to use it if I'm in urgent danger."

They all sit in silence, looking at the stone for a minute, having no clue as to what it might do.

Gidjie continues, "I know how to barter with animals, and how to barter with humans on behalf of animals," as she talks, she feels less worried about what they might think. Based on the looks on their faces, everything she is good at, are things they don't know how to do themselves.

"Sounds like you're bringing a *lot* of good things to the council," Onie says, smiling at her, "Hey, want to see something?" she asks Gidjie, motioning down to her hand that's resting on the ground between them.

One finger shortens, becoming covered in black fur. A little claw appears on the end.

Onie looks super proud, "I haven't told my parents about this yet. It's kind of a secret," she says.

"What else are you?" Gidjie asks, genuinely impressed to see Onie has the ability to take more than one animal form, if even just a finger.

"I don't know yet," Onie admits, noticeably a little embarrassed by that fact, "All I know is, it likes to dig," she says, pointing down to her hand again, where the one little finger is digging at the soil while the rest remain flat on the ground.

"Just the finger?" Roze asks, leaning in, not having heard the entire conversation.

"Yeah, so far," Onie says.

"My aunt has two forms. She says with each comes different responsibilities," as soon as Gidjie says the word 'aunt,' she feels like her inner world's about to crumble.

The rest of them all sit quietly, uncertain about what the future holds and whether or not they will be ready to do what is needed of them individually and as a council.

A few moments of silence pass, and when Gidjie is near bursting into tears, Roze breaks the silence, "So… what do you all suppose we're here for, specifically?" he asks the group.

"My aunt Molandoras and the wolves she studies are missing and I'm afraid she's been taken…maybe by humans," Gidjie blurts out.

"Oh no, that's awful!" Onie says, trying to comfort Gidjie with a hand on the back while Gidjie pads a few tears away on the sleeve of her dress.

The energy in the council chambers shifts from casual to concern.

After a moment, "We're going to find your aunt," Zhee declares optimistically.

"He's right," Onie says, "this has got to be why we've been called." She looks at Gidjie, "We're going to find her."

Gidjie does her best to stop sniffling and nods her head.

"How do we find missing wolves?" Roze asks.

"Well, if we were looking for them in their own territory, I'd know approximately where to look," Gidjie says, "My aunt has been studying them for years in the Boundary Waters Area. But if they've been moved, and presumably, caged," she can't believe she is about to suggest this, "then we need to track down the humans responsible."

"Did you all arrive here in the tunnels?" Zhee asks.

Everyone nods 'yes.'

"Well, I flew here," he says, smiling big, "and so was able to see that the Great Beaver Pole Lodge is *in* the Boundary Waters," Zhee informs the council.

"Well then we need to go, like right now!" Gidjie says, jumping to her feet.

"It's going to be okay, Gidjie," Roze says, in a voice calming enough to make her take a deep breath, "Is there anything else we should know?"

Gidjie exhales. After one more round of deep breathing, she feels steadier, "Well, there's six members of the wolf family," she tells the group, "Assuming they've all been taken, there had to have been a transportation vehicle. Someone must have seen or heard something; the forest is full of eyes."

There's a minute of silence.

"We're a council now; and we know why we've been called," Carver addresses the group, "What do we do first?" his gaze comes to a stop at Gidjie.

Gidjie looks around the circle, and again her eyes water. This time, it's not because of Molandoras. It's because looking around at all of them, she knows they really are here to help.

"Like Zhee said, we're already in the Boundary Waters Area. We need to start by asking people around the lodge if they know anything about any wolves, foxes, snakes or humans, before we go running off on a wild goose chase," she says.

"She's right," Zhee says in his duck voice, "wild gooses can be hard to catch."

It takes only a moment of everyone looking at Zhee, and then around at each other, before once again, the council chamber is ringing with laughter.

Owl Hears a Howl

"Well," the spider starts, "I don't know anything about wolves. We haven't had any stay with us for a while, probably 'cause they got a nice den of their own, just that way," she says, pointing with 6 of her 8 legs out a small window, indicating a ways down the shore to the east, "I suggest you ask Long Ear, the owl; he lives near there."

"Where can we find Long Ear?" Roze asks her.

"He's overseeing lodge construction," the spider says, shooting a thread up to the ceiling, and in an instant, she is upside down, weaving with all 8 of her legs in a near blur. Gidjie recognizes the material she's making; it's what the door curtains and bed linens are made of.

The council leaves the spider's linen room and continues up the hallway that is now bustling with beavers and muskrats of all sizes and temperaments.

"Excuse me," a mid-sized beaver says, pushing their way through the middle of the council.

They turn to watch him trot off casually down towards where their council chambers are. As they are turning back around, a very large Intermediary beaver jumps up to scare them, "Hey! Watch where you're going, kids!"

"Ah!" Roze exclaims, surprised, "Hey, real funny," he says to the beaver, who smiles contentedly with himself as he makes his way around the council to their left.

Following the beaver, comes a rush of a half-dozen, small, full-time muskrats, scurrying between their ankles silently. Gidjie's foot hangs in midair, as one rushes underneath it.

"Lunch time!" a larger muskrat says, lifting up his hardhat made of ironwood to the council and running past them on two legs while rubbing his stomach. Gidjie recognizes this last muskrat is also an Intermediary.

At the end of the hallway, they emerge into the daylight and open air of a beautiful, sunny day. They look around. There's only water and forest for as far as they can see—and they're standing right in the middle of the large, earthen structure that is the Great Beaver Pole Lodge. The surface of the lodge is enormous in itself, and they know it's just the tip of the iceberg.

"Wow, this beaver lodge is huge!" Onie exclaims.

"Hey, over there," Carver lip-points to an inconspicuously sized owl, who's hopping around on a low-lying, wooden table about 40 paces away.

"That must be Long Ear," Gidjie says, seeing no other owls around.

The council makes their way in his direction; Zhee, Carver, and Roze roughhousing in their animal forms along the way.

By the time they have reached the owl, he has begun snoring with his back towards them, head tucked into his feathers. Wasp paper maps are strewn about the table and are held down by river stones to keep them from blowing in the wind.

"Excuse me," Gidjie says to the owl.

He opens his bright yellow eyes, blinking one, then the other, and then unravels his head a full 360 degrees, startling the council, who all take a leap back.

The owl smacks his beak sleepily. His feathers puff up as he squints at them, "What do we have here?" he asks, "A new council?"

"Yes, we are," Gidjie says, "Are you Long Ear?"

He looks from one council member to the next, and can't help but ask, "Why are you two humans? Look kind of funny, don't you think, two young humans on the middle of a beaver lodge, talking to old Long Ear?"

Gidjie is about to say something apologetic about being human, but instead steps closer, "Wouldn't it look just as funny for an owl, an opossum, a wolverine, and a duck to be talking to each other, regardless of if there's a human among them?"

"Indeed," Long Ear smiles, "What can I do for you, young council?"

"We're wondering if you've seen anything unusual, or heard of any missing wolves, foxes, or snakes?"

Long Ear is quiet for a moment, his feathers puffing up again, and then flatten quickly, as he remembers, "I did hear something. Three nights back, I heard the strangest wolf-howl. I couldn't get it out of my head. I decided I had to go and discover what had happened."

Long Ear turns away from the council and scans the water, "There," he says, pointing to the edge of the southern side of the water in the distance, where there is a hard-to-see opening in the wood line, "that's where I saw a green pickup truck pull away with a large cage on a trailer. I didn't see what was in the cage, however, as

146

the humans had tied a tarp over the top with bright yellow cloth rope before I arrived."

The council exchanges worried glances.

It's then that Gidjie notices four large eyes, blinking at them from within a small tunnel in the lodge just a few steps away.

"We saw them," a voice says from the darkness.

"We saw them tooked," a second voice follows the first.

Two Frogs
in a Froggy Hole

Tell a Tale

"Grub woke one day in a place that was dark and filled with a delicious smell.

"'What's that?' he wondered with delight.

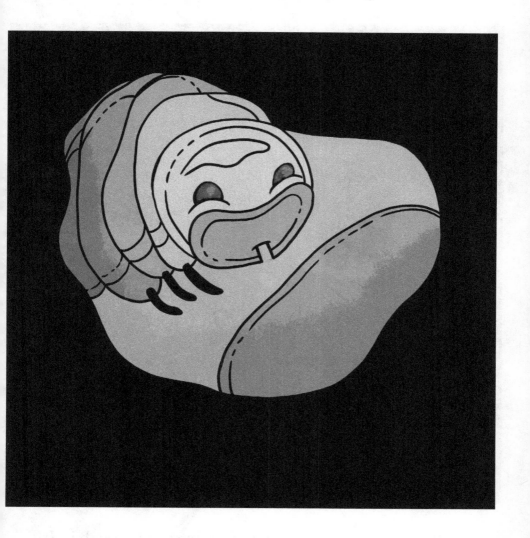

"He found that he had a mouth, and so he ate and ate until he consumed the entire source of deliciousness.

"After a while, he had grown so big that his body filled the darkness. It was then that he noticed the tiniest flicker of light.

"'What's this?' he wondered, trying not to touch it. It was hard not to, because his body was now pressed up against a solid surface that was holding him in place.

"It was uncomfortably tight in the darkness, but he was very full and content.

"He decided it best to leave the light alone, and so he went back to sleep.

"Grub slept for a long time.

"He woke to a cracking sound.

"'What's that?' he thought to himself.

"He realized it was him that had caused the sound, as he was pushed against the side of his world.

"With another moment, his head broke through the darkness and into a bright wide open.

"'Now, what's this?' he asked again, peering around into his bright, new world.

"He tried to pull his head back into his cozy home. He pulled so hard, that his rear end crashed through the other side. He could feel a draft on his rear.

"'What's that?' he asked, as he tried to look around the edge of his shrinking home to see what his rear was doing.

"That's when he caught wind of a delicious new smell.

"It came from just ahead. He forgot about his exposed rear and stretched his neck out as far as he could, trying to get to the smell.

"He stretched and he stretched, but he could not reach the smell.

"He stopped stretching.

"Instead, he looked up, down, and all around at the old word he was stuck in. It was smooth and brown, and the bottom was unmoving on the soft surface upon which it sat. It was a good world. Grub didn't want to leave it behind.

"'What's this?' he asked, looking down at the surface beneath his home, as he wanted to move towards the new smell.

"He tried rocking back and forth while pulling his head, and then his tail end, back and up and forward and down and in and out, until...

"*Pop! Pop! Pop! Pop! Pop! Pop!*

"His tail had swished forward so hard, that it was sucked back into the shell, while his head had come up so high, that it drove six legs down through the bottom of the snug-for-a-grub home.

"'What are these?!' he exclaimed, as he watched them wiggle about.

"Again, he smelled the most delicious and new smell he had ever smelled.

"He found his new legs allowed him to move forward and he sought out the source of the smell.

"Beetle was very happy with this arrangement. He could keep his old, safe world while exploring his new, bigger one that had much to enjoy," the big, bright green tree frog Intermediary on the right says, finishing up the tale.

"What's the moral of the story?" Zhee asks, both entertained and confused.

"No mo-rel, only bee-tel," the tree frog on the left says.

"I mean..." Zhee begins, and then adds, "never mind," thinking it's not very good manners to question the lexicon of a storyteller.

"No morel, only beetle shell," the frog on the right says, rubbing her belly with her eyes closed, like she was remembering a disagreeable taste, "Big beetle shells are no good for eating," she continues, "but big beetle shells make good bins," and she disappears for a moment.

When she returns, she's holding a very large, old beetle shell above her head. It's full of fishing lures.

"I have to snip them and grip them and flip them...into here," she says, "The more I snip, the less *they* come. The less they use my children... as bait."

"Where are your children?" Roze asks.

The frog on the left motions out towards the water.

"Is there anything you remember about the humans who had the trailer? The ones Long Ear mentioned?"

"We snip and snip and snip from them. Then they go," the frog on the left says, and digs around in the lures for a moment, before pulling one out and handing it to Gidjie.

"Hey, I recognize this fish!" Zhee says, snatching it out of Gidjie's hands, "Sorry," he tells her.

"Well, what is it? Where do you recognize it from?" Carver asks him.

"It's a mailbox!" Zhee exclaims excitedly.

Roze flattens his eyes out and says, "That. Is a mailbox? Zhee, you're losing it."

Zhee gives Roze a 'what?' look and turns back to Gidjie and says, "No. But it *looks* exactly like a mailbox we fly over every year on our migration south," he says, "Hmm. I wonder if I'll be migrating this year, now that I'm part of a council…" he trails off in thought.

"A mailbox?" Onie interrupts his self-talk, "So, you know exactly where this came from?" she asks him.

He turns the lure sideways in his hands, careful to not snag himself with the hooks. It is a fish that is brightly colored red and looks like it's been hand carved. He looks at the bottom and reads, "M.E.," and his eyes get really big, "This is also on the mailbox! And, to answer your question, Onie—I sure do!" He pauses for a second, "Only, I'm not sure how to get there on foot from here, which is what we'll need to do collectively; but we should start at the site Long Ear pointed out."

Zhee then turns to the frogs, "Thank you!" he tells them both, and turns to the council, "Let's go!"

The Approach

"We need to gather more supplies," Gidjie says aloud, looking into her empty food sack.

"Supplies?" Onie mumbles through a mouthful of young, tender leaves; little bits of green plants sticking out of her mouth.

"What kind of supplies?" Zhee says between gargles, while swimming alongside them. He does a tail stand in the water and then pulls his head back up and gulps down a little fish.

Opossum Carver runs ahead to where Roze is.

I wonder what Roze's human form looks like, Gidjie thinks to herself, realizing she's only seen him as a wolverine, as of yet.

Carver and Roze begin digging beetles out of a rotten stump.

Looks like everyone has food, for now.

It's then that she remembers the little piece of dough that had somehow managed to get out of the jar and stuck to the seed.

She looks around to make sure none of the council can see into her bag, before peeking down into it.

The seed is alone. There is no sign of the dough. There's not even a dried, crusty spot on the seed where it had been stuck. She hurriedly checks the rest of the bag. It's not there.

She shuts it quickly, not wanting anyone—especially Carver—to know she's been reckless with the little dough-ball.

I can't believe I lost a piece of Bluebelle, she thinks, feeling extremely guilty.

"I see a road!" Carver alerts the rest of the council from just ahead.

When Gidjie catches up to him, she sees the road is narrow and unpaved. There are plants growing up between muddy tracks that indeed look like those of a pickup. Her heart feels heavy.

How could anyone take Molandoras? Why? Why would they trap the wolves? The foxes? The snakes? If they knew her; if they knew the animals…they wouldn't have done it—would they have? Gidjie swallows hard, trying to keep from getting choked up.

"Everyone keep your senses peeled, for any signs of humans," Onie says.

"Particularly any smells," Zhee says, looking at Gidjie and pinching his nose teasingly.

Gidjie's throat relaxes a bit and she tries her best at a comeback, "Hey, ducks are smelly too," she says, giving him a friendly shove, the both of them laughing off the stress of the situation.

After another hour and a half of following the dirt road, Gidjie is getting quite hungry. She's just starting to think *I wonder what those beetles Carver and Roze were eating taste like…*

When Roze calls from up ahead, "Hey, the road splits up here!" and then, "Hey, I found berries!"

Gidjie loves berries. She makes it to Roze and sees there is indeed a split in the road. She looks around the area and finds oodles of little three-leafed clusters that have tiny, deep-red strawberries hiding underneath. She eats them as quickly as she can get them off of the stems.

Carver joins them. It doesn't take long before all of the council are gathered around, eating the berries.

After fifteen minutes or so, Gidjie is feeling less hungry and sits down. She takes out a little pinch of asemaa and puts it under one of the strawberry plants, whispering, "Please, if you could, have pity on us. I don't know if my heart can take not finding my aunt, or her not being okay. If you could help us find Molandoras... please help us. Miigwech."

She stands up, "Hey, look," she says, pointing up to a marker in a tree just above where she was sitting, "it looks like the yellow fabric rope Long Ear saw tied to the trailer.

The council looks around the area where the road splits, "There's more down here," Roze says, trotting off in brisk wolverine fashion.

"There are signs posted that this is private land," Carver tells Gidjie, as they walk fast to catch up to Roze.

"If that's the case, and they've marked the area, then they might live nearby," Onie says, "or at least have a cabin here."

"Maybe Molandoras is there, too," Gidjie says, her heart racing. She begins to run. They all do.

The council spends about an hour following the markers until they come to what looks like a smaller trail forging into a thick grouping of pines.

"This is the place," Zhee says, "It looks different from the ground, but this is it, I know it. I can feel it. I can feel it right in my compass."

"Compass?" Roze asks.

"It's like an organ that tells us ducks how to migrate."

"There's an organ for that? What is it—the gizzard?" Roze says and starts laughing.

"I'll gizzard you a reason to laugh," Zhee says, flapping up to sit on Roze's shoulders. He nips at the fur on the back of Roze's neck with his bill. They roll around for a minute in a laughing scuffle.

"Hey, you two, quiet down," Onie says from just ahead of them, "I think you might be right, Zhee. I can see a building up there."

The sun is beginning to set.

The council is quiet as they walk down the trail, approaching the scary unknown.

After a couple of minutes, the thick pine forest opens up on the left, revealing a house and two outbuildings in a clearing.

"Do you hear that?" Onie asks.

They stop to listen.

It's four-wheelers. They're out of sight but approaching fast on the main road.

"There!" Carver says, pointing to a fallen tree in the brush to the right.

They make it behind the tree in time to see two four-wheelers, each with one person, growl up the trail and pass them on their way towards the house. One of the four-wheelers has a trailer attached to the back, but there's nothing on it.

"This is it, look," Zhee says, pointing at a mailbox attached to the wooden railing on the front porch of the house. Gidjie has to squint, but she is surprised to see it is indeed a red fish.

The quickly darkening forest provides cover, as the council makes their way closer for a better look. They stop when they are just on the other side of the trail, across from the house.

Gidjie can see 'M.E.' is painted in bright white paint on the side of the mailbox.

"That's weird," Onie says with a look of confusion on her face, "I don't think that mailbox is for regular mail. There's no way a mail person would come all the way out here. It's probably for some other kind of deliveries."

They watch the house for over an hour from the tree line. The men start a fire in the front yard and sit around it, drinking beer and talking quietly. Occasionally, they shout profanities at each other and then laugh.

Gidjie stares helplessly at the doors of the outbuildings, which face towards the fire, the men, and the woods that are providing the council with cover. The buildings are windowless, making it impossible to see what's inside of them.

Gidjie touches her necklace, wondering about what could count as 'urgent danger,' "I think we should set up camp for the night," she says, realizing how tired her feet and every other part of her is from walking all day, "I really want to know if Molandoras is here, but we can't get into those buildings until they're sleeping," she says, talking about the men. She pauses before deciding it's important to be more outspoken, "Actually...I can feel her," she looks around at her council, "She's here. And she's alive."

The rest of the council looks hopefully to Gidjie.

"That's what we were hoping to hear," Onie says, "She's okay. She's going to be okay," she repeats. Gidjie can tell Onie is saying this to calm herself down. It seems to calm everyone else, too.

"So...you have a compass in your gizzard too, aye?" Zhee asks Gidjie.

She can't help but smile at him, "Something like that."

The council agrees that they should make camp. They walk farther into the woods behind them, until reaching a small drop down where a few fallen trees are scattered about.

"This is good," Roze says, knowing that they're out of sight far enough to not be seen from the trail, even in the daylight.

Onie curls up, as a small deer does, under the branches of a low-bowing pine tree. Zhee beds down into some leaves on the ground nearby.

Gidjie wedges up to one of the fallen trees, while Roze and Carver settle down atop one of the others.

Gidjie barely has time to think, *I'm glad it's a warm night,* before she has fallen asleep.

A little while later, she's awoken by quiet giggling. She lifts her head just enough to determine the source. It's Roze and Carver.

"So, you've known her your whole life?"

"Yep. Not even a day I don't remember seeing her. Well...except for when I knocked her grandmother into a honey bucket."

Roze stifles his laughter, and then says, "Was she okay?"

"Yeah," Carver chuckles, still embarrassed by it, "But yeah, there was this one time, Gidjie ate these roots that made her sleep for a week—twice, actually, she did that—but I still saw her every day. The first time, I was worried she wouldn't wake up. The second time was just as bad, really."

"Sleeping for a week? That's scary."

"Yeah, it was."

"You just sat there watching her?"

"I talked to her. I thought it might help."

Gidjie suddenly feels guilty for not being asleep *now*. She hadn't meant to eavesdrop on them.

She lowers her head. *Carver always made it sound like it was no big deal. He never told me he talked to me while I was sleeping. If it was the other way around, and I was worrying about him, I'd probably be mad at him for making me worry. But I probably wouldn't want him to feel bad about it. Am I too hard on him sometimes? Do I tease him too much?*

Gidjie realizes the conversation she is having in her head, with herself, is the kind that she's never had with Carver, or anyone, for that matter. She usually just brushes those kinds of thoughts off and doesn't *really* talk about how she feels or ask Carver how he feels either.

I can't wait to talk to Molandoras, is her last thought before falling back asleep, craving a widening in her ability to communicate.

Captured

Carver wakes to the sound of a quiet-rumbling engine on the approach.

He climbs a tree, high enough to see a four-wheeler coming to a stop on the trail. He quickly scurries down and makes his way to the edge of the woods.

The four-wheeler is parked. A tarp covers something sitting on a hitched trailer behind it. There is no sign of the driver. A second four-wheeler pulls up behind the first.

Carver backs up slowly into the brush line.

To his horror, the first man appears from behind a large pine tree just feet away, zipping up his pants.

Carver drops 'dead.'

Moments later, the man is standing over him, "Got a dead one over here," he says, giving Carver's motionless body a lift with his boot, rolling him over onto his other side, "I think I'll pass on this one." The man laughs, then walks away.

Carver opens his eyes to see the man standing by the side of the trailer. He lifts up the tarp to show his friend something.

It's Roze. And his mouth is bound with rope.

Oh no, oh no, oh no, oh no. What were you doing by the road? Carver thinks, panicked but still laying as dead-like as he can. Roze sees him through the bars of the cage.

"Might as well drop this one off first," the man says, pulling the tarp back over the cage.

Carver picks himself up as the first man gets on the four-wheeler. He looks to the campsite where the rest of the council remains sleeping. He doesn't have time to wake the others *and* climb under the tarp before they pull away.

Refusing to lose sight of Roze, he climbs onto the trailer just as it begins to move.

Gidjie wakes with a light covering of dew on her dress. She rubs her eyes and looks towards the fallen tree that Carver had slept on, "Carver?" she calls out quietly. The tree is bare. There's no sign of Carver or Roze.

"I think something is wrong," Onie says, having woken just before her, "Come, look at this."

Zhee is up on his duck feet, rubbing his eyes, "What's going on?" he says, yawning, "Where's Roze and Carver?"

They follow Onie to the trail where she points out some scuffle marks in the dirt and freshly made four-wheeler tire tracks. She then points over to the larger building, where the four-wheelers are parked outside. A cage sits empty, door open, on a trailer behind one of them.

Gidjie's heart beats faster than it ever has.

Why is this happening? she thinks, tearing up and angrily wiping the tears away. *What could they possibly want with Molandoras, the wolves, the foxes, the snakes—and now my very best friend in the whole world?*

A Skunk with a Plan

Gidjie, Onie and Zhee are crouched between a bush and the small garage. Their eyes are glued to the door of the larger outbuilding, where the men have been inside for about ten minutes.

"I have an idea," Onie says.

Gidjie looks to Onie and her jaw drops.

There, instead of Onie-the-deer sitting beside her, was one very surprised but determined-looking skunk.

"You're a skunk?!" Zhee says, nearly too loud from the other side of Onie.

"Shh," she whispers, her finger in front of her mouth, "I hear something."

There's a rustling in the bushes behind them.

Gidjie catches a glimpse of a small form, "It's not a human," she's relieved to tell them.

An Intermediary badger approaches them, "On the fourth and twelfth days of the moon, the truck is gone till after noon," he motions to the small building beside them, which houses the pickup.

Gidjie, Onie and Zhee look at each other, unsure of what the badger's rhyme means.

"Today is the twelfth day of the moon," he illuminates, before continuing on his way. He looks around cautiously for signs of the men, before disappearing behind the building.

A sapsucker flies just inches over Gidjie's head and disappears behind him.

"Who was that?" Zhee asks, "Do either of you know that badger?"

Gidjie and Onie shake their heads 'no.'

"He apparently knows who we are though, or at least has an idea of what we're up to," Gidjie says.

"So, we wait until they leave, and then make our move?" Zhee says.

"Onie, you said you had a plan?" Gidjie asks her.

"Well...I think we should hold off on my plan for now. We should wait until they leave. We'll use mine as plan b, if we have to."

"Well, what is it?" Zhee really wants to know.

"Plan b is literally, plan *b*," she says, throwing her butt in the air, her striped skunk tail sticking straight up.

"Yesss!" Zhee says, genuinely excited to have skunk power on their side.

"They're leaving," Gidjie calls attention to the building, where the men are pulling the door shut. They get on their four-wheelers and start driving straight for the smaller building.

The three quickly move backwards into the brush.

The men stop on the front side of the building, and one gets off his four-wheeler. Moments later, a pickup pulls out. The men drive the four-wheelers in to the garage, and then the sound of the pickup begins to move away, getting quieter as it disappears down the trail.

When they can no longer hear the truck, Gidjie shouts, "Now!" She can't see anything else in the world but the door, as she races as fast as she can towards it.

Onie the deer is the first to reach it, "No! It's locked!"

Breathing heavily, Gidjie pulls and pushes on the handle. It doesn't budge. She starts pounding on the metal door, "Molandoras! Carver! Roze! Can you hear me?!"

A noise comes from the other side of the door. And then it opens. It's Carver.

"Carver, you're alright!" Gidjie hugs him around the neck until he squeaks.

172

"I'm okay, really," he says, "I snuck in here. But Roze is still tied up. I was just about to grab the keys," he says, walking to the side of the door where a ring of keys hangs, "These are just for the smaller cages, like the one they put Roze in. Molandoras said they keep the ones for the rooms in the house."

"Molandoras is locked in a room? Where?!"

Carver runs Gidjie to where Molandoras and the wolves are being kept, before running off to free Roze. Zhee stays at the door to keep watch, while Onie investigates the rest of the building.

"Gidjie?" the voice of Molandoras sounds from behind her.

"Auntie!" Gidjie turns to see her aunt in human form, gripping the bars on a small window in the door. She can only see Molandoras' hands and face. She looks disheveled. Gidjie bursts into tears, "Why did they do this to you?" she sobs, grabbing Molandoras' hands.

"Gidjie, you have to get the keys," Molandoras says, "in the house. You have to go now, quickly."

Gidjie doesn't want to leave her side. She cries uncontrollably at the sight of her aunt in this condition.

She stops when she hears Zhee yelling.

"Do you hear that? It sounds like—oh no, the pickup!" he shouts, peeking through a small crack in the door. "We gotta do something," he tells Onie, who had come running at the sound of his yell.

"Looks like it's time for plan b," Onie says.

"I was hoping you'd say that," Zhee confesses, and then hollers, "Gidjie, we gotta go, now!"

Gidjie runs out the door past them in a sprint as the sound of the truck gets louder.

They reach the porch and Gidjie enters through the unlocked front door. Zhee runs around to the back of the house.

"Here goes nothing," Onie says, giving the porch a good spray before making her way behind the house, just as the truck to comes bouncing into view.

The man coming up to the house is mumbling under his breath at the other man, who still sits in the truck, "…next time, lock the door…" is all Onie can make out.

"Wait for it. Wait for it," she's whispering to herself.

The man reaches the walkway to the house and stops. He makes a face. He walks a little closer and stops again. He tries a quick trot towards the porch, but the smell is so powerful that he turns back around and runs to the truck.

The two men yell at each other for a minute.

Inside the house, Gidjie holds her breath, looking out between the curtains in the living room, one hand over the stone of her necklace. She gets a good look at the man's face before he runs back to the truck. She begins breathing again as the pickup backs out of the driveway quickly, kicking up dirt as it peels out onto the trail.

A knocking at a window in the back of the house gets Gidjie's attention. She runs to the sound and sees Onie and Zhee jumping up and down.

Gidjie opens the window, "I was so scared," she tells them, "What happened? Why did they leave?"

And then she smells it.

Skunk spray is pouring into the back window as the wind changes, "Nevermind," she laughs, "you two are the best."

"Did you find the keys?" Zhee asks.

"The keys!" Gidjie turns from the window and frantically begins searching the house. Onie climbs in to help look while Zhee waits under the window, keeping watch.

Onie finds Gidjie in the kitchen, grabbing the keys off of the table where there also lies a pistol, a newspaper, and a lighter, "This place gives me the willies," Onie says.

"Come on, let's go," Gidjie tells her, and runs back to the window where Zhee is waiting. She climbs out the window.

"Get ready to run!" Onie hollers from inside the house. In a moment, she is her human self, climbing out of the window then bounding away quickly as a deer.

"Ah, wait for us!" Zhee shouts, as skunk spray begins oozing out of the window.

"Who're you?" Gidjie asks a kid about her age, who's sitting next to the door of the outbuilding rubbing their jaw, their long brown hair in a messy braid, "Were you trapped in there, too?"

They look up at Gidjie with bright golden eyes, "Gidjie, it's me, Roze," he says.

Gidjie stares at him for a moment, and then smiles, "I didn't know what you look like, until now," she says, "I just didn't realize you…"

Roze laughs, "It's okay, I get it. All this pretty confuses people. It's why I don't usually walk around like this."

Gidjie smiles, "I'm so glad you're okay, Roze," she tells him, and holds out her hand to help him up, "I like your pretty," she says. Roze blushes a little, and then turns into his wolverine self and takes off trotting inside.

Gidjie tries several keys before finding the right one.

"There are cameras all over," Molandoras says, walking out stiffly with a slight limp.

Gidjie hugs her tightly.

Molandoras points one out in the corner of the hallway, "They must have them up in the trees, too." She becomes quiet. She lowers her head, "I think…they must have seen me with the wolves."

Gidjie's eyes bulge in worry, "You mean they saw you…changing?"

"I don't know for sure, but why else they would have taken all of us? They must not have known which wolf was me, so they took us all until they could figure it out."

"This is bad," Gidjie says, and looks around at the council, who had gathered around Molandoras. Three pups, at least one a fox, trots by them on their way out of the building, "We have to destroy all of the cameras here."

"That…might not be a problem," Onie says, looking anxiously over her shoulder.

"Whaddya mean?" Roze asks.

"Well…I didn't know there was water in that bucket. Or that there was a power strip right below it. Or that it would start on fire if it got knocked over."

Zhee's standing next to her, nodding his head and pointing at her with his thumb, "She's not kidding, this place is gonna be lit up, we gotta get outta here."

"Oh no. Is everyone out?" It's then that Gidjie looks over the shoulder of Molandoras, who's still in the doorway of the room she'd been locked in.

The wolves stare at Gidjie so intensely that she loses her breath. She grips tightly to Molandoras' arm.

The two of them move into the hallway and the rest of the council makes space for the wolves to exit.

"That's everyone, I think," Onie says, after the wolves have evacuated.

"We have to keep looking, Gidjie, we haven't found any snakes yet," Carver insists.

Gidjie nods her head, "Zhee, Onie, you go with Molandoras and Roze to wait outside. Carver and I will look for the snakes."

Smoke comes billowing down the hallway from the back of the building.

"Okay, let's go!" Zhee asserts, flapping his wings behind everyone to get them moving.

Gidjie and Carver run up and down the building.

All of the cages are empty.

And then Gidjie sees something shiny on the lower part of a wall in one of the rooms, "In here!"

It's a large glass terrarium that's set flush into the wall.

"Pull on that end," Carver says, taking the other side. They slide the terrarium out into the room. It's full of snakes.

Gidjie gasps.

"We can't leave them here," Carver says, after realizing the terrarium is too heavy to carry, "Move back!"

Carver unlatches the top and a waterfall of snakes cascade out.

"Carver, those are rattlesnakes!" Gidjie backs up as quickly as she can, "Come on, let's go!" she shouts before turning and running towards the door.

Gidjie watches from the grass as snakes pour out the front of the building and disappear into the brush line nearby.

"Carver!" Gidjie yells at the door when she realizes he wasn't right behind her.

He stumbles out, holding his furry opossum arm, "One of the little ones got scared and..." he moved his hand to reveal a snake bite.

"Oh no," Gidjie drops to her knees to steady him, seeing he's woozy.

"Don't worry, I just need a minute and I'll be okay," he says, falling onto Gidjie.

"Help! Onie, Roze, Zhee, please, help!" She cries, dragging Carver farther away from the building as smoke begins to engulf it.

The rest of the council leaves Molandoras nearby and runs over to see Carver drooped across Gidjie's lap.

Wolves begin to howl from the forest just out of sight.

"What happened?" Roze says, turning into his human self and dropping down on one knee to check Carver's vitals.

Onie and Zhee look at him in surprise, and then they smile, seeing his human form for the first time.

"He was bit by a rattlesnake," Gidjie says through sobs.

"That's all?" Onie says, matter of factly.

Gidjie shoots daggers at her with her eyes.

"He's an opossum. They can get bit and be okay," Onie adds quickly.

They all look at Carver, who is looking nearly dead.

He breathes in a gasping breath, and then motions them to come in closer with a weak paw. They do.

After a long, exaggerated breath he says, "It-th true," his tongue hanging out of his mouth, his eyes closed, "opothumth have a thnake therum in their blood," he says, unmoving, "I'm not in pain, but I can't theem to move for the time being. Jutht give me a few minuteth."

"What's a thnake therum?" Zhee puzzles.

"Snake serum," Onie clarifies.

Gidjie smiles through her tears, "Carver, you nearly gave me a heart attack! Had I known this *before* you dove at that cage full of rattlesnakes..." she then stops her scolding and embraces her friend with her happiness, his floppy tongue and rolled-back eyes and all.

Family

There is silence other than the squishing of shoes, dragging of tired paws on earth, heavy breathing of Carver, and the occasional duck sneeze, as the council, Molandoras, and the three diverse fox pups pad their way down the dirt road towards the Great Beaver Pole Lodge. A smoke plume grows tall above the forest behind them, coming from the building that has nearly burnt to the ground.

"Cripes, I've got mud in my bill crevices," Zhee says, followed by another sneeze-quack that sends little mud bits flying in all directions.

"Can I ask you a question?" Gidjie says, helping Molandoras walk along.

"What's that?"

"Do you know anything about…time travel?" Gidjie says, embarrassed.

"I might," Molandoras replies without hesitation, startling Gidjie, "but I wouldn't call it time travel. It's more like light travel. Although, certain people have figured out how to alter the time that's associated with the light. As far as I know, you can only alter time in one direction—forward, and I'm not the kind of person who could ever leave anyone behind," she stops walking to stare firmly at Gidjie, "I hope you're not that kind person either. That's all I have to say about that."

"But…"

Molandoras puts a hand up to her mouth, indicating silence, "You're on a good path. Don't lose course for anything," her brows furrow, "or anyone."

"Hey Gidjie, you wanna come over to my house?"

Gidjie turns to see Onie grinning at her.

"In the city?" Gidjie's throat tightens, her eyebrows raise an inch in embarrassing but uncontrollable fright.

"We'll have a lot of fun," Onie says, "And maybe now that we're part of a council, mom will let us help with her investigations."

Molandoras squeezes Gidjie's hand, "You'll be fine," she says, "Maybe she can help you learn about your human family."

Or…I can find out more about the men who took you, Gidjie thinks.

"Sure," she says, smiling at Onie, "why not?"

"What about us?" Carver asks. The three boys are staring at Onie.

"I guess we need to find a headquarters for our council," Onie says to them all, before, "A vehicle's coming," alerting the group.

They scramble to the side of the road.

"It's Nookomis!" Gidjie cheers.

"Nookomis to the rescue!" Zhee yells, waddling his duck self towards the bus that's now stopped.

The door swings open and the council piles in, introducing themselves as they enter.

Gidjie helps Molandoras up the first step. Before she gets on herself, she catches movement from the tree line. It's the pups. They run behind the long legs of a large, red fox. Gidjie nods at them and they cheerfully trot along, nuzzling one another and playing as they go.

"You came," Gidjie tells Nookomis with much appreciation as she climbs to the top of the steps. She gives her grandmother a hug.

"I had the itch," Nookomis says, smiling.

Gidjie notices there's something different about her ears. She leans in for a better look and Nookomis says, "These babies can hear as far as the moon now."

Gidjie laughs, not sure if Nookomis is joking or not.

184

"Oh," Nookomis says as Gidjie walks past her to take a seat, "Mino stopped by. Seems you left something in his company. Said he could bring him by when we get home."

Carver and Gidjie look at each other, "Him?" Gidjie thinks out loud, "The only thing I've lost while I've been gone is...." she gasps, "the dough!" Gidjie's head is in a spin, as she walks back to take a seat.

"Come on, I'll take everyone home. Carver, your basket is in the back," Nookomis says, lifting her sunglasses up to peek at the council in the rearview mirror, before replacing them back on her nose, "There's plenty of goodies in it for everyone."

"Goodies!" Zhee yells excitedly, and then begins to sing, "Gram-maaaah, where's the goo-dies, goo-dies. Goo-dieeees, where's the gram-mah, gram-mah."

Before long, the joyous singing of different animals can be heard pouring out the windows of the bus, as it rolls down the dusty road; windows down, heart strings blaring; right on tune, right on time.

About Gidjie and the Wolves

This book was inspired by a series of animal dreams the author had between the winter of 2017 and the winter of 2018. The dreams featured a family of wolves, dancing foxes, tree frogs, a large spider, and others.

Thank you
for spending time in the world of
the *Intermediaries*

Next in the series:
"Gidjie and the Island of Moon"

Visit the author's website:
Tashiahart.com

Instagram:
@tashiamariehart

Twitter:
tashiahartbooks

Acknowledgements

To my husband, Jonathan Thunder, who always encourages me to embrace my creativity and go all the way with my endeavors—I truly couldn't have finished this book if not for your love, support, and ace inking skills. Chi-miigwech niwiidigemaagan.

To the handful of family members, friends, colleagues and mentors, who have read my work over the years, cheer me on, and give me valuable insight (with special thanks to Marcie Rendon, Linda LeGarde Grover, Heid Erdrich, and Christina Woods)—nimiigwechiwendaan indinawemaaganag.

This book was made possible with the help of a 2019 ARAC Career Development Grant; I am ever so grateful for your support.

Tashia Hart (Diindiisikwe) grew up in the wilds of Northern Minnesota. She loves animals, writing, drawing, plants and cooking. "Gidjie and the Wolves" (*Intermediaries*, volume 1) is a combination of the things she loves.

She is Red Lake Anishinaabe.

Jonathan Thunder (Manidoo Gwiiwizens) is a member of the Red Lake Ojibwe Nation. He practices as a multi-disciplinary artist, working in canvas painting, animated films and illustration.

Thunder has been the illustrator of multiple picture books, including: Naadamaading, Deer Woman: A Vignette, Every Child Deserves, Anooj Inaajimod, and Bowwow Powwow, which earned Best Picture Book in the 2020 American Indian Youth Literature Awards.

To learn more about Jonathan's work, visit: thunderfineart.com